LIAM O'CONNOR IN

"THE KEY TO
BETRAYAL"

JOHN MATTHEW LEE

"Liam O'Connor in 'The Key to Betrayal,'" by John Matthew Lee. ISBN 978-1-62137-843-3 (softcover).

Published 2016 by Virtualbookworm.com Publishing Inc., P.O. Box 9949, College Station, TX 77842, US. ©2016, John Matthew Lee.

ACKNOWLEDGMENTS

I wish to personally thank the following individuals for their contributions and support (without which, this book would never been written):

My wife, Kelley, and our two sons, Kevin and Thomas

My mother, Connie

My sister, Grace

Jerry

Stella

Michael

Sandy, my longtime canine companion

I appreciate each and everyone's input in the writing of this book. You each gave me a piece of your time and helped me reach a longtime goal. I'm humbled, and will always be in your debt. Thank you all!

Table of Contents

CHAPTER 1
DÉJA' VU

"YOU HAVE THE RIGHT TO REMAIN SILENT. Anything you say can and will be used against you in a court of law. You have the right to talk with a lawyer and have him present with you while you're being questioned. If you cannot afford to hire an attorney, one will be appointed to represent you before and during questioning, if you desire. If you give up your right to remain silent, and later wish to stop answering questions, no further questions will be asked. Do you understand each of the rights I've explained to you...Mr. O'Connor? I need an answer," says Lieutenant Tibedoe.

Liam sits thinking, I must have read suspects their rights a thousand times, and yet never fully felt the importance of each right... how odd. It's unsettling to think how your life can change in a minute. Choices made by you, or for you, can change your life's path. Hours earlier,

I sat in my condo watching old black and white movies. No longer seeing or feeling in color like in my youth. I see and feel in black and white, through foggy eyes. Where has the color gone? Everything's different now.

"Mr. O'Connor. I need an answer," says Detective Lieutenant Tibedoe.

"I understand the rights you've read to me. Am I under arrest?" asks Liam.

"Not at this time. We're just trying to figure out what the hell happened here," says Lieutenant Tibedoe.

"Me too! Me too, Lieutenant Ty-bow," says Liam.

"It's Tibedoe," replies his partner, Detective Anthony Molina.

Liam looks over and sees a slight smile from one of the uniformed officers in the condo.

"Between the detectives, uniformed personnel, and crime scene technicians, you would have thought I was giving away pizza and beer," says Liam with a slight grin.

Liam looks outside and notices several of the neighbors standing, watching, and waiting to see or hear something that could carry them through their week. Something that would break their dull, daily routines.

"Liam...Liam, will you talk to me?" asks Lieutenant Tibedoe.

"Yes, I have nothing to hide. I too want to know what the hell is happening," says Liam.

"Let's start from the beginning," says Lieutenant Tibedoe.

"Yeah, that's always the best place to start," says Liam in a tired and slight Bostonian accent.

"Do you have some form of identification?" asks Tibedoe.

Liam takes out his driver's license from Boston and puts it on the table. Lieutenant Tibedoe is called away from the dining room by a crime scene technician.

"Your full name is Liam Matthew O'Connor, and you are currently 57 years old. Is that correct?" asks Detective Molina.

"That's right," says Liam.

"It shows that you lived in Brighton, Massachusetts, as of three years ago when you last renewed your license. Is that right?"

"Yes."

Liam notices a grouping of officers in his bedroom, along with Tibedoe, going from bedroom to bedroom.

"Is Sandy okay?" Liam asks.

He gets no response, so he starts to stand and walk toward the office when Molina says, "Hey, what are you doing? Sit down... sit down, you're not free to get up and wander around. You need to stay put!"

Lieutenant Tibedoe calls Molina to the bedroom. Detective Molina tells a uniformed female officer to stand by Liam and to not let him move from the table. As Molina walks away, Liam yells out,

"What the hell is going on? You guys act like this is your first homicide or something."

Officer Youngblood turns to Liam and says, "Sir, we've only had two homicides over the past six years that I know of. Now we have two dead bodies in one night. I'm not sure what the chief is going to think of this."

"Is Sandy okay?" Liam yells out. "I need to check on Sandy."

Officer Youngblood asks if Sandy is Liam's wife. Liam doesn't answer.

"I'm going to check on her," says Liam.

Officer Youngblood tells Liam, "I'll see what's taking the lieutenant so long."

She walks to the bedroom and slowly enters. A short time later, she sticks her head out and says, "Is Sandy your dog?"

"Yeah, she's my seven-year-old, sixty-five pound boxer," says Liam.

Officer Youngblood says, "She's fine, she's sleeping on your couch with her bone."

Detective Molina and Lieutenant Tibedoe return to the kitchen bar counter, along with Officer Youngblood and several other uniformed police officers.

"Liam?" asks Tibedoe. "Why didn't you tell me you were a cop?"

"I'm retired now," says Liam. "I retired eight months ago from the Boston Police Department after serving thirty-three years on the force."

"That explains it, Tee," says Molina.

"Explains what?" asks Liam.

"It explains why we have two dead men on the floor of your office, both shot twice in the head and chest, and you're not even the least bit nervous," says Detective Molina.

"Hey, Skippy," replies Liam, "I'm nervous, and somewhat confused, but this is not my first time being involved in a shooting where people have died."

Lieutenant Tibedoe looks at Liam and says,

"It looks like, from the photos on the wall, you were a detective at one time."

"That's right," says Liam. "I worked fifteen years as a patrol officer and sergeant, mostly in South Boston. My last twenty years I worked in the Detectives Bureau, retiring out as a homicide lieutenant. I'm sure you saw a few pictures in there. You see now,

Skippy," he says, looking at Detective Molina, "not my first rodeo."

"Got it," replies Detective Molina. "I also saw a wall covered with high school football team pictures."

"I had a life away from work sometimes. I coached football for my alma mater, Brighton High School, for some twenty years after I finished playing at Boston College," says Liam.

Lieutenant Tibedoe notices there are several pictures of the same two ladies that looked to be mother and daughter, both having long, flowing red hair and green eyes. Lieutenant Tibedoe asks,

"Is this your wife?"

pointing to a picture on the wall. Liam gets up from the table, walks over to Tibedoe and looks at the picture, takes a deep breath and says,

"That's my daughter and wife. That picture was taken in front of Fenway Park."

Tibedoe asks, "Where's your wife and daughter now?"

"Are you divorced?" asks Molina.

Liam replies, "Is this part of the investigation?" looking at both Molina and Tibedoe.

"I live here alone," says Liam.

"Look, detectives! I would really like to go down memory lane with the two of you, but are these the questions you want to ask me? I think not."

Detective Molina, Lieutenant Tibedoe, and Liam walk back to the table and sit down. Liam sees that Officer Youngblood has walked out of his office and has Sandy by her collar.

"Hey, where are you taking her?" asks Liam.

"Relax," Tibedoe says.

"I'm just taking her outside until all the processing is finished," says Officer Youngblood.

"Her leash is on the hook by the back door," says Liam, looking surprised.

"What's the matter?" Molina asks.

"That's only the second person, other than myself, who's been able to get close enough to walk that dog."

Tibedoe asks, "What brought you to Port Saint Lucie, Florida? Long way from Boston."

"My mother," says Liam. "My mother moved down here several years ago, after my father passed. She wanted to get away from the winters of Boston. At eighty-three, she lives in an assisted living community near the Wanamaker Club. If something was to happen to her...I'm all that's left of the family. My brother, James, was killed in '71 in Vietnam."

"Do you work, or just enjoy the retired life?" asks Lieutenant Tibedoe.

Liam looks around his home, watching the crime scene technicians and the coroner's personnel loading up and removing a body from the bedroom.

"Enjoying retirement? This is bullshit! I left Boston to help simplify my life. I work, if you can really call it that, at the Wanamaker in the golf shop as a starter, a few hours a week...really, it lets me keep a routine. Dave lets me play golf for free."

"When did you start working at the Wanamaker?" asks Tibedoe.

"I started about six months ago, but Dave, the golf pro, will have the exact date of the start of my employment. Something tells me the two dead guys weren't disgruntled golfers, Tibedoe," says Liam.

"We don't have a clue who they are at this point. Do you?"

"No, I don't recall seeing those faces. But there were so many cases for so long, I can't be sure," says Liam. Detective Molina leaves the table and works his way back to the bedroom, out of sight of Lieutenant Tibedoe and Liam.

"Liam, tell me what you did today, up until the time of the shooting," says Tibedoe.

"Okay, okay. I was scheduled to open at the club this morning, which means I got to the Wanamaker about five a.m. and opened up, and worked the counter till about noon. It was early in the afternoon when I got off work, and then I had lunch at the club before I came home."

"Is this one of those private high-dollar golf courses?" asks Lieutenant Tibedoe.

"You don't play golf, do you, Ty-Bow?" asks Liam.

10

"No, basketball is my game," replies Tibedoe.

"This is a public course, open to all classes. Even you could play, if you had balls... and clubs, of course," says Liam. He thinks, of all the luck, I get a new detective who I have little in common with. I hate basketball. I'm probably the only white Irish Catholic Boston native who's never played hockey or basketball.

"What time did you get home?" asks Tibedoe.

"It was about two in the afternoon when I got back to the condo and checked on Sandy. I took her for a walk around the complex for about forty minutes or so, and then we headed back just before four. I remember that because Boston College was playing USC on ESPN, and I wanted to see the game," says Liam.

"Did you see anybody on your walk or during the day that was suspicious to you?" asks Tibedoe.

"No. It was just a regular Saturday afternoon," says Liam.

"Liam, what happened then?" asks Tibedoe.

"I watched the game till around seven-thirty or so when it ended. I began to watch an old war movie when I fell asleep. I guess around nine o'clock. I awoke hearing the rain outside, just after eleven. I took the dog out and let her do her thing, while I stayed on the back covered patio."

"Did you see anything, anybody, any suspicious vehicle that didn't belong?" asks Tibedoe.

"No," replies Liam. He thinks, have I lost those skills that came so easy to me at one point in my life? Oh Lord, not now... don't do this to me now. Shit.

"Tibedoe, you must have a good memory. I haven't seen you write down shit since you read me my rights," says Liam.

"Got it covered," says Tibedoe, pointing to a digital recorder he had placed on a cabinet near the table. Liam looks at the recorder and at Tibedoe, and briefly smiles, like a proud father.

"I haven't been able to sleep through the night for probably twenty-plus years." says Liam.

Molina asks, "You mean you have to piss several times a night?"

Liam looks at Detective Molina and says, "You know, Molina, you're kind of a dick, but I guess you can't help that. Incompetence will cause a person to speak before they think sometimes!"

Tibedoe smiles and says, "What happened next, O'Connor?"

Liam says, "I have bouts of insomnia, and I awoke about two or so in the morning and began to watch a movie. I was watching a movie when Sandy got out of the chair. We were in the office, not in my bedroom, so I got up and noticed it was still raining out, with flashes of lightning. I thought the dog got spooked, so I called her back to the office. I noticed she started to growl. That's when I retrieved my gun from the cabinet in the office. Sandy doesn't usually growl unless someone's outside. I got my gun, and at about the same time I heard the slider door to my bedroom being opened. I looked to see where Sandy was, when the next thing I knew, I heard subjects inside the bedroom and saw them walk toward the hallway. I was in a kneeling position in the office. The TV was on and the volume was down low."

"Did you hear either of the subjects say anything as they entered through your bedroom slider door?" asks Tibedoe.

"No, I wasn't sure how many subjects there were at that time. I remember thinking it took them a little time to get from my bedroom to the hallway. The first subject entered the office and scanned the room as the second subject followed. Both subjects had semi-auto handguns in their hands, and as the first subject continued to scan the office, he saw me. That's when I fired two rounds at the first intruder, and two rounds at the second."

Tibedoe asks, "Did the second subject point his gun at you?"

"I remember he had the gun in his right hand, but I don't recall where he had it pointed at the time I fired," says Liam.

"Liam, that accounts for four rounds fired, total. But we know you fired eight," says Tibedoe.

"That's right," replies Liam. "I fired again, until they stopped moving. I guess old habits are hard to let go. I fired two shots toward the subject to my left, sweeping back to the first subject. I fired two more rounds into his head, or so I thought."

Tibedoe asks, "What do you mean?"

"I wasn't sure how many times I hit the subjects, only that I must have hit them both, because they stopped moving. I moved from my position to theirs and removed the guns from their hands. I scanned the condo for additional subjects and looked outside to see if I saw anyone leaving from the parking lot area, but I only saw lights coming on in the complex," says Liam.

"What did you do then?" asks Tibedoe.

"I found my cell phone and called 911, and told the dispatcher that I'd shot two armed subjects who had just broken into my condo."

Tibedoe asks, "Did you do anything else before the first officer arrived?"

"No, I just waited and noticed more and more of the neighbors' lights come on, and then heard sirens approaching. I looked outside and saw my neighbors looking toward my place... and that's it," says Liam.

"That's it? That's it, you didn't do anything else?" asks Tibedoe.

"No," replies Liam.

Liam thinks to himself, there is no need for him to know that I checked both of the subjects for any signs of life, hoping to ask questions, but both were dead with bullet holes to their faces and foreheads. Chuck, the Boston Police Rangemaster, would have been proud. He continued checking the pockets of the subjects and found only one had anything on him. He had an envelope containing ten hundred-dollar bills and a small piece of paper with Liam's address on it. Neither subject had a wallet, identification, or keys... nothing. Liam also did a quick examination of the bodies as he continued to hear sirens and saw more and more lights come on in the neighboring condos. He saw that both subjects were white, well dressed, and had several tattoos on their arms. Some were military in significance, and others were not. Liam knew his investigating time was running out. He removed a second cell phone from his office and took several photos of both subjects, just prior to the first officer arriving on scene. He then placed the cell phone in the attic above the hallway crawl space.

Liam examined the subjects' weapons and noticed both carried semi-auto

Glocks with laser sights, and the serial numbers from both guns had been removed.

"Okay, Liam, is there anything else you want to tell us?" asks Lieutenant Tibedoe.

"What do you mean?" asks Liam.

Detective Molina answers, "Do you mean there's nothing else, or just nothing else you want to tell us?"

"I have nothing else I can think of at this time, but if I remember something, I'll sure let you guys know," says Liam.

Lieutenant Tibedoe reaches over, turns off the recorder and says, "Liam, this sure is a strange burglary, if that's what it ever was." Liam looks at both detectives and says nothing.

Liam asks, "Where is Officer Youngblood? Does she still have Sandy?"

Detective Molina replies, "She's still outside with the dog."

"Am I free to go outside now?" Liam asks.

Tibedoe says, "Liam, we're done processing the place. We may have more questions in the future, but we know where to find you."

Liam starts to go to the patio door to check on Sandy when in from the outside rain comes Officer Youngblood and Sandy.

"Thank you," says Liam, looking into the eyes of Youngblood, then down at Sandy, who just sits and looks up at the both of them.

"She's not usually so friendly toward people. She usually keeps away from most folks."

"Well, you can never tell why dogs see things in certain people," says Officer Youngblood.

"My wife used to say that," says Liam. He takes the leash from Officer Youngblood and lets Sandy loose into his home.

Lieutenant Tibedoe says loudly, "We're done here. Check your gear, let's go, everyone, wrap it up."

All police personnel begin to file out of the condo, along with members of the county coroner's office. Liam sees that both detectives are near their vehicles talking to their chief and other department personnel, when Mrs. Sandrini looks at Liam standing near his front door and says, "What happened?"

Liam replies, "Rats! I've got problems with rats."

Mrs. Sandrini looks over at the coroner's body removal van and says, "Seems like the problem was taken care of."

Liam says, "I wish it was that simple."

Liam continues to look outside and watch the detectives by their vehicles. That's right, don't even search the neighborhood or check the parking lot for possible suspect vehicles. We wouldn't want to do any real detective shit here, would we, thinks Liam. He checks his home and as he thought, his gun and spare magazines were seized by the Port Saint Lucie Police.

"It's all right, Sandy," says Liam. "Seems I've become relevant again to someone, but to who and why?"

He knows this was no robbery or burglary gone bad. This was a hit attempt. Liam also knows that it won't be long before whoever sent these two would send more, until the task is completed.

"Lieutenant Tibedoe, did you see the citations from the Boston Police Department for valor and bravery in his office?" asks Molina.

"Yeah," says Tibedoe, "along with many more commendations over a thirty-year period."

"There were even more in a drawer in the closet, along with several photos of O'Connor in uniform and as a plain-clothed detective," says Officer Youngblood.

"Is that right?" says Molina. "What were you doing checking the closet?"

"It's all right," says Tibedoe.

"I was looking for a dog leash," Officer Youngblood replies angrily as she walks away.

"What do you think?" asks Lieutenant Tibedoe.

"It looks like a professional hit attempt to me," says Chief Green.

"You said that both dead guys had no ID on them, nothing but an envelope containing money and O'Connor's address? O'Connor told you the subjects entered through his back slider and immediately began searching for someone? They weren't looking to steal. They came for O'Connor," says Chief Green. "But why?"

"You need to find out more about O'Connor," says Chief Green. "See me in the morning, and I'll give you the number of Deputy Superintendent Finnegan of the Boston Police. He and I went to the FBI academy together several years ago. He's Deputy Superintendent of Personnel. He might be able to help with O'Connor. He might give you a little more background on him."

"Thanks, Chief," says Tibedoe. "Anthony and I will see you when we can get the autopsies done. Maybe we can identify these guys, then that might tell us something."

"Okay, that sounds good. Sometime, you and Officer Youngblood should go talk to O'Connor's mother. She might give you some background on her son."

"Okay, Chief. Since you have more experience in murder investigations than I do, is it normal for a person to show little to no emotion after killing two people?" asks Tibedoe.

"Who's to say what's normal?" says the Chief. "People process things differently. I killed in combat. In war it bothered me at first, and then it didn't. I did what I had

21

to do, just to get through the day. O'Connor fits the type," says the Chief.

"What type?" asks Molina.

"The type of man who's at the end of his rope, someone who doesn't give a shit about anything anymore, just trying to exist from day to day."

Officer Youngblood returns back to Lieutenant Tibedoe's location and states, "I've checked with the neighbors to see if they heard or saw anything suspicious prior to the shooting. I got nothing. No one saw or heard anything."

"Good work," replies Lieutenant Tibedoe. "Detective Molina, would you be so kind as to have yourself and several of the patrol officers do vehicle registration checks of all of the vehicles in the complex? See if you can account for all of them. These assholes got here somehow!"

"Yes sir, Lieutenant!" says Molina.

"I'm taking off, Tibedoe. Call me if you have something tonight. Otherwise, I'll see you in a few hours," says Chief Green.

He begins to walk to his vehicle, and after a short distance away, Lieutenant Tibedoe says to Officer Youngblood, "I told you, never date someone in the workplace."

She looks at Tibedoe and says, "What do you mean?"

"It's obvious that you and Anthony aren't seeing eye to eye," says Tibedoe.

"We aren't dating anymore," says Youngblood.

Lieutenant Tibedoe shakes his head in disgust.

"Anthony," he says. "Anthony! Of all the people in the department. Officer Tina Youngblood, you're better than that," says Tibedoe. "Don't you watch Oprah?"

Youngblood looks up at Tibedoe and says with a smile, "I get cold at night, too."

Detective Molina returns to Tibedoe and Youngblood and says, "Tee, it's going to take several hours to get this done. I mean, there are a lot of vehicles in this complex."

"Welcome to homicide, Anthony," replies Tibedoe. "Let's get on it."

Officer Youngblood and the detectives continue to search for any vehicles that might have been left behind by the suspects, but after several hours of checking registrations, all vehicles in the complex were those of the residents.

Tibedoe says, "We're done here. Go ahead and clear."

Tibedoe looks at Molina and says, "Be back at the station by noon. We've got autopsies to schedule, and a lot more follow-up to do."

Liam continues to watch Lieutenant Tibedoe and the other officers search the complex for foreign vehicles. He calls several cab companies stating that he and a friend had been dropped off earlier at the Lake Charles complex and would like to be picked up by the same driver, but just couldn't remember the cab company's name. He tells the dispatchers they had been drinking and are a little out of it. After several cab companies say they have no record of a drop-off earlier at that location, Paradise Cab Company tells Liam they have a record of one of their drivers having a fare earlier in the night from the airport to that location, and would they like him to return for a pickup. Liam tells the dispatcher not at this time, but that he would call in a few hours after they sobered up. He looks at his watch. A few more hours, and T.J.

should be working. He sits down in his favorite chair and thinks, who wants to fuck with me now, and why? He dozes off to sleep as Sandy lies beside the chair.

CHAPTER 2
MAMA O

"WHAT, NO COFFEE?" Lieutenant Tibedoe asks Molina. "Tony, you look like shit!"

"Hey, I got maybe three hours of sleep before I'm back in the office again. How come you look so good? You got about the same amount of sleep," says Molina.

"I guess I just need less beauty sleep than you," replies Tibedoe. "The Chief wants us in his office in ten minutes to brief him on what we've got so far, before he meets with the press."

"What do we have?" asks Molina.

"The autopsies are scheduled for 13:00 hours today. I need you to attend and let me know if the coroner can identify either of the subjects, and what criminal history comes up on them, if any," says Tibedoe.

"I'm on it," says Molina.

Officer Youngblood enters the detectives' office and hands Molina a piece of paper with the name Issaic Rodriquez written on it.

"What's this?" asks Tibedoe.

"This is the cab driver at Paradise Cab Company who drove two subjects to O'Connor's place early this morning. You were right, sir, they took a cab. The owner of the company said Rodriquez will be into work at 22:00 hours tonight. He said that Rodriquez works the night shift and picked the two subjects up from the airport at around midnight, and then took them to Mickey's and was told to wait a few minutes until they left the bar, and then drove them out to O'Connor's complex at around 01:00 hours or so.

"He said the fare was paid in cash."

"Good!" says Tibedoe, "good work, Youngblood. You and I will go speak with O'Connor's mother. She's staying near the Wanamaker Club at the Carriage House. It's an assisted living place."

"Hey Tee, why does she get to go with you, and I have to do the autopsies?" asks Molina.

"Tony, I need a woman to be with me when I talk to Mrs. O'Connor. It just might be easier for her to talk, and Tina has never gone to an autopsy," says Tibedoe.

"Got it," replies Molina.

After briefing Chief Green on their current status with the case, Lieutenant Tibedoe and Officer Youngblood drive to the Carriage House to meet with Mrs. O'Connor.

"Mrs. O'Connor, my name is Detective Lieutenant John Tibedoe, and this is Officer Tina Youngblood. We're with the Port Saint Lucie Police Department. We'd like to talk to you about your son, Liam, if that's okay with you?" asks Tibedoe.

"Is Liam okay?" asks Mrs. O'Connor in a soft Boston Irish accent.

"Yes, ma'am," says Officer Youngblood, "he's fine."

"Ma'am, there's been a bit of trouble at your son's condo earlier this morning, and we were hoping you might provide us with some information that could help us in this investigation," says Tibedoe.

"Investigation into what?" asks Mrs. O'Connor.

"Ma'am, earlier this morning two individuals entered your son's condo, armed, and tried to kill him. However, Liam shot and killed them. When we made contact with Liam, he didn't appear to be too disturbed by what had just happened," says Lieutenant Tibedoe.

"I see," says Mrs. O'Connor in her soft voice, "but Liam is okay...right?"

"Yes, ma'am, he's fine," says Youngblood, "and his dog was unharmed as well."

"Well that's good. That old dog means a lot to him these days," says Mrs. O'Connor.

"Ma'am, it doesn't look like Liam did anything wrong, but these guys weren't there to rob or burglarize. It looks to me like they were there for Liam," says Lieutenant Tibedoe. "Do you know why someone would want to harm your son?"

"My son was a homicide investigator with the Boston Police Department for over twenty years. He worked as a lead investigator for about fifteen years, and then as a lieutenant before he retired. I don't know how many people he put in jail for murder, but I can tell you two things for sure. One, in his entire time in homicide as an investigator and lieutenant, he never had an unsolved murder.

And two, the Boston Police Department just about killed my boy!" says Mrs. O'Connor. "I was never so glad as to see my son retire. I thought I would get a call from Kelley one night telling me Liam was dead, shot down on the job, but as it was, I got a call from Liam telling me he lost Kelley in a traffic accident on I-90. After Liam lost Kelley, he left the department."

"Ma'am... Kelley, was that his wife?" asks Youngblood.

"Yes, Liam and Kelley were married for thirty-four years when she passed. She was a music teacher," says Mrs. O'Connor.

"I think we saw a picture of her, and of their daughter," says Tibedoe.

Mrs. O'Connor points to a picture of Kelley, Liam, and their daughter Molley, and says, "That was his wife and daughter. Molley lives in Atlanta now. She's a human resource manager for a big Catholic hospital."

"That was them in the picture," says Youngblood.

"Molley is not close with her father. She blames Liam for the death of her mother. You see, Liam was to drive Kelley to a school function the night Kelley died. Kelley was the music teacher at Brighton High School, and Liam was a coach for the football team for over twenty-five years. He was known at the school as Coach O. Kelley had a concert, and usually Liam would drive Kelley to her activities if it meant driving in the snow or wet weather conditions on the interstate. Kelley didn't like to drive when there was snow on the ground," says Mrs. O'Connor.

"Liam was to be off work by five o'clock that day, but was working overtime on a homicide call out. Molley blames her father for not being there, not driving Kelley to the school, and I think Liam blames himself too," says Mrs. O'Connor.

"Would the two of you like a cup of coffee?" asks Mrs. O'Connor.

"Please," says Officer Youngblood. Lieutenant Tibedoe looks at Youngblood with some surprise and asks, "You said earlier that you weren't happy with the

Boston Police Department's treatment of your son. Why?"

"Well, Liam, like his father Joseph, loved being a cop. After the Korean War, Joseph became a cop in Boston. He worked the streets for thirty years. He retired, and he and a few friends bought a bar. He worked at that old neighborhood bar until he died of a heart attack several years ago. So you see, Liam is a second generation Boston cop. His father didn't want him to be a cop. He always thought Liam would be a football player. He was an outstanding football player at BHS and earned a scholarship to Boston College. The day Liam went to college, Joseph was one proud father—proud that his son was at Boston College, and proud that he was playing football. Since Liam was a boy, he always wanted to be an Eagle, but Liam had a hard time making the team," says Mrs. O'Connor.

"I think he realized his talent level was only going to take him so far. He injured his knee his first year at college, and the damage so bad he couldn't play football again. The college pulled the scholarship after Liam's freshman year, but he continued his schooling," says Mrs. O'Connor. "Liam worked as an orderly, while going to college, to help pay for his schooling. I had hoped he would have become a doctor. He seemed to like the work at the hospital. But he and Kelley wanted to start their life together, so Liam became a police officer like his father."

"Ma'am, why didn't your husband want your son to be a police officer?" asks Officer Youngblood.

"Well, I think he wanted better for Liam. I know I didn't want him to join the force. I now had to worry about my husband and son not coming home from work on any given day...it was really difficult for me, but I prayed and believed that God had a plan. In the early days, Liam's father worked the streets in the South Boston area on foot. You know, certain parts of Boston are pretty rough. Gangs of all colors were working to take control of areas of Boston. It was a rough time for the Boston Police Department," says Mrs. O'Connor.

"Mrs. O'Connor, do you have any idea who might want to harm your son?" asks Tibedoe.

"I don't know, I just don't know. Liam keeps so much to himself," says Mrs. O'Connor.

"Thank you for your time, ma'am, we'll be going now. Here's my card. If you have any further information that might help us, please call me," says Lieutenant Tibedoe.

Lieutenant Tibedoe and Officer Youngblood leave the Carriage House and return to the station. Once back at the station, Chief Green meets with both Youngblood and Lieutenant Tibedoe at Tibedoe's desk,

"Well, John, did you get anything from Mrs. O'Connor?" asks Chief Green.

"Yes sir, we got some background on her son and what he did for the Boston Police Department, and what happened to his wife."

"John, while you two were out, I called and spoke with that friend of mine in the personnel department of the Boston Police Department. His name is Deputy Superintendent Finnegan," says Chief Green. "He told me some interesting things about your man Liam."

"Is that right?" asks Tibedoe.

"He said he and Liam's father, Joseph, came on the department at around the same time. He said Joseph worked the streets most of his career and never wanted to be promoted within the department. He said he was a tough old Irish cop who loved the streets and wasn't afraid to bust some heads. He worked the streets for his entire career, right up to the last day on the job. Finnegan told him that it's pretty common for the older cops to get off the streets, but it was no surprise that Joseph didn't. If there was ever a cop who loved the streets of Boston, it was Joseph. He just figured Joseph would have completed his entire career on the streets. Finnegan said Liam's old man was a cops' cop! He also told me that Liam was a chip off the old block. That early in Liam's career, he worked the streets and was involved in several shootings, in which he helped save many officers' lives. He said according to his personnel file, Liam received over seventy commendations for outstanding work, and three medals of valor for bravery. Liam was promoted to detective sergeant and moved into the homicide unit after about eight years on the streets." Chief Green continues to say that, "Finnegan said Liam had been shot in the line of duty some six or seven years ago, while trying to arrest a homicide suspect. He was shot through the front door of a third-floor apartment with a twelve-gauge shotgun. Liam returned fire and advanced into the apartment, where the suspect was killed."

"John," says Chief Green, "the suspect was killed by Liam, with two shots to the head and two to the torso. Deputy Superintendent Finnegan also told me that Liam had shot, and killed, four potential homicide suspects during the course of his career. He said the last shooting O'Connor was involved in, he was hurt pretty bad. He thought O'Connor lost his spleen and several ribs, along with parts of his intestines and stomach. He said the department was prepared to medically retire Liam, but after several long months of rehabilitation, along with a clean bill of health from the department's psychologist, he returned to work."

"O'Connor received three medals of valor awards, but also received days on the hook without pay," says Chief Green.

"What do you mean, 'days on the hook'?" asks Officer Youngblood.

"What he means is O'Connor got suspended several times. But for what?" asks Tibedoe.

Chief Green says, "The shootings were ruled outside of department policy, as Liam was found to have fired more than the recommended shots into the head of all the suspects."

"So let me get this straight," says Tibedoe. "The Boston Police Department was praising O'Connor for his outstanding work on the one hand, and then disciplining him with suspension days on the other."

"Yep, that's right," says Chief Green. "Finnegan said there were many in the command structure that didn't like the public and media attention O'Connor brought to the department. Apparently O'Connor had a dislike for most of the command staff of the Boston Police Department."

"Chief, Mrs. O'Connor told us her son never had an unsolved homicide case," says Tibedoe.

"Well, Deputy Superintendent Finnegan said that during Liam's time as a lead homicide detective, that was correct. In fact, he remembered the Chief Commissioner and command staff brought that little-known fact out for the media from time to time. He said it got to be quite the dog and pony show. John, Finnegan told me one last thing. He said Liam had requested a special assignment to the FBI academy. The FBI had asked if Liam could be used as an instructor at their national academy. They wanted him to teach a class on interview and interrogation techniques, but the department wouldn't loan him out for a year as requested," says Chief Green. "It's likely this guy has been miles ahead of you on this entire investigation."

"Well if that's so, Chief, maybe he'll do our work for us!"

"Yeah, you're right, but how many bodies are we going to have to pick up along the way?"

"Lieutenant Tibedoe," Officer Youngblood says. "I wrote down several names of medications I located in the bathroom of O'Connor's place last night, but I've not heard of any of them."

"Why did you do that?" asks Tibedoe.

"Well, sir, there was a bottle of medication near the sink, and I went to put it up when I noticed all the rest of the medication with his name on it. I

39

thought there was a lot of medication for just one person, so I wrote them all down," says Youngblood. Chief Green looks at John in a surprised way.

"Good," says Tibedoe. "I'll call Doc Hill. He'll know what the medications are used for."

"I thought," says Youngblood, "that O'Connor's place was so neat and organized, and to have a bottle out on the bathroom counter seemed almost out of place. That's what drew my attention to it. I know that seems kinda stupid," says Youngblood.

"No it doesn't," says Chief Green, "that is what we call developing your cop instincts. It appears to me, Officer Youngblood, you've got good instincts when it comes to investigations. You keep up the good work."

"Thank you, sir," replies Youngblood.

The phone rings at Mrs. O'Connor's room at the Carriage House.

"Mama, it's Liam."

"Hello, Liam. The police were here earlier today," says Mrs. O'Connor.

"I thought so," says Liam.

"Are you okay, son?"

"I'm fine, Mama. I guess they told you what happened?" asks Liam.

"Yes!" answers Mrs. O'Connor.

"I've got to figure this out, but until then, I want you to stay at the facility. I'll keep in touch, Mama," says Liam.

"Son, what about Molley?"

"She doesn't need to know anything about this. No need to tell her anything right now, Mama. What could I tell her? I'm going to call T.J. and see if he can help me," says Liam.

"Oh, you tell T.J. I miss him, and he needs to come and see me soon," says Mrs. O'Connor.

"You tell T.J. I'll cook him his favorite meal if he comes to see me."

"Chocolate cake too?" asks Liam.

"Cake too," replies Mrs. O'Connor.

"Goodbye, Mama."

Liam hangs the phone up and says to himself, "Chocolate cake is my favorite, not T.J.'s."

CHAPTER 3

DUTY, HONOR, FAMILY

LIAM DIALS THE PHONE NUMBER of his closest living friend, Tyrone Johnson O'Leary.

"Hello," answers T.J.

"Is this Mr. Tee-rone Johnson O'Leary, the famed athlete of BHS?" asks Liam.

"Liam, it's so good to hear your voice. How are you doing?"

"I'm fine," says Liam. "It's good to hear your voice too, T.J. I hate to call and bother you, but I need your help on something."

"What is it, my brother from another mother?" asks T.J. "What do you need?"

"T.J., last night I had a couple of visitors try and kill me. I didn't recognize either of these dung-heads, but I thought that if

I sent you a couple pictures of these guys along with some pictures of tattoos from their arms, you might be able to run the info through the criminal database and identify them," says Liam.

"Liam, what's going on?" says T.J.

"I don't know, T.J., why would anybody need to get to me now? I haven't been with the department for almost a year now. T.J.," Liam pauses, "they came for a reason. I'm sure it has something to do with Boston," says Liam. "Can you help me without getting in trouble? I'll e-mail the photos I took with my cell phone. The local coroner here in Port Saint Lucie will probably attempt to identify these guys through their prints through the Department of Justice. I'll bet they have prints on file, either with the Department of Justice or the Department of Defense," says Liam.

"Do you think they were ex-military?" asks T.J.

"One had some military type tats on his upper arms," replies Liam.

"Liam, if they're in a system, I'll find out who they are."

"T.J., don't let anybody know that you've talked to me. I don't have an idea yet where this is going to lead me. For now you're safe, and I want to keep it that way. Your e-mail is still the same, right?" asks Liam.

"Yes, it's still outside the department on a private server," says T.J.

"Will you be the only one that has access to it? I don't want to drag your wife into this shit too! She'd have my ass if she knew I was getting you involved in my shit again," says Liam.

"Liam, send it to me now. It will be fine," says T.J.

"Okay." Liam sends the photos via e-mail.

"I'll let you know something as soon as possible," says T.J.

"Okay ... I owe you one, again. Call me back on this phone number. It's clean."

Liam ends the phone call with T.J. and thinks to himself, I don't want to get T.J. involved in my mess.

Liam has always looked upon T.J. as another brother. He remembers how he first met Tyrone Johnson O'Leary. A freshman at Brighton High School in Boston. Both trying out for the football team, Liam as a linebacker and T.J. as a running-back. It wasn't long before they were the best of friends, even though they were from very different backgrounds. Liam, a white Irish Catholic from the South Boston area whose father was a Boston cop, and T.J., who lived with his grandmother and mother who had been in and out of jail for drug-related charges his entire life. T.J. had never known his father, but had dealt with many men who had come and gone. During T.J.'s freshman year in high school, his grandmother passed away. His mother was serving time for drugs and prostitution charges, and he found himself alone. Liam brought T.J. home to stay, and without a thought, Liam's mother and father took Tyrone Johnson O'Leary into their home and told him he could stay as long as he wanted.

Joseph O'Connor believed in never looking down on another man, unless you were helping him up. His service in the Korean War had profoundly changed his views of people. Joseph O'Connor was saved many times in the war by soldiers of color. His view of racism became clear early in life. He judged an individual's worth by their actions, not the actions of others of similar color. Tyrone Johnson O'Leary came to live with the O'Connors his freshman year in high school, and left to join the Marine Corps six years later.

At the Port Saint Lucie Police Station, Lieutenant Tibedoe is on the phone saying, "That's interesting. Are you sure those drugs and the daily doses would only be prescribed for that, Doc? Okay, thank you, Doc."

Lieutenant Tibedoe hangs the phone up, turns to Officer Youngblood and says, "Those drugs you wrote down in O'Connor's place? Dialect, Depraved, Symmetry, and Enshrinement. The doc says those drugs are prescribed for someone in the early stages of Parkinson's disease.

Those drugs are supposed to control tremors in the extremities. So it appears our man Liam has Parkinson's disease, but it's in the early stage." He looks to Officer Youngblood. "Has anyone heard from Anthony?" he yells as he looks around the detective division for a response. "I'm going to call him. Have they got our guys identified yet? I mean, I know how they died, shit!"

Several hours pass before the phone rings at Liam's home.

"T.J., is that you?" asks Liam.

"Yeah, it's me. I've got some information on those two guys. I was able to identify them from their photos and tats. You were right, Liam, the dark-haired subject had several military tattoos on both of his upper arms. The Department of Defense has identified him as Daniel Scott Shea. Shea was 32 years old and did six years in the Army," says T.J. "Liam, he did three tours in Iraq and one in Kosovo as an ammunitions specialist. He was honorably discharged three years ago out of Fort Bragg, North Carolina."

"Has he had any arrests since his discharge?" asks Liam.

T.J. pauses and states, "Yeah, he's been arrested on misdemeanor assault charges several times over the last two years, but never convicted. He's out of Charlestown, Massachusetts. He's a townie, Liam," says T.J. "Yep, that's right!"

"I know the Sheas out of Charlestown had connections with the Irish mob, but I don't think I ever had a case involving a Shea family member," says Liam. "T.J., who is the other guy, the lighter complexioned guy?"

"His name is Bobby Dale Pentacost. He has an arrest record a mile long. Everything from possession of drugs to assault with a deadly weapon," says T.J. "He was on parole for weapons violations out of West Virginia."

"Did you say Pentacost?" asks Liam.

"Yeah, that's right. Bobby Dale Pentacost, twenty-nine years old."

"Shit!" says Liam. "Is there any listed family on his arrest and booking information...anything?"

"Do you know this guy, Liam? Did you arrest him or something?" asks T.J. "He lists his mother as Connie Pentacost, last address listed on his arrest information was in Wheeling, West Virginia. "Do you know Pentacost?"

"I think in 1990 or 1991, I worked a homicide involving some brothers with the last name of Pentacost. I'll have to check my murder books again," says Liam.

"You still have copies of all your cases?" asks T.J.

"I have a copy of every case I ever worked as a detective. Even some I worked as a lieutenant," says Liam.

"Don't get yourself in trouble accessing the computers from the Department of Defense. If an audit is done, you need to cover your ass. T.J. ... you could contact Pentacost's parole agent and inform him of Bobby Dale's death. That way if you're questioned, you could say you were assisting another department. That may work."

"Liam, you let me worry about that. If this leads you back to Boston, remember, I've got your back," says T.J.

"Thanks for sticking your neck out for me, brother. I've got to go. I'll keep you up to date with whats' going on if I can. Bye," says Liam.

"Tony, this is John. Have you got anything for me yet? You've been over there for the last four hours. Has Doc Hill identified them yet?" asks Tibedoe over the phone. Then he explains to the chief what Molina is telling him over the phone. "Tony's got them both identified. The light complexioned one is a parolee out of West Virginia named Bobby Dale Pentacost, and the other is Daniel Scott Shea, last known address out of Charlestown, Massachusetts."

"John, Doc Hill said that Charlestown is a suburb of Boston. I think you and the chief were right. This is some past baggage of O'Connor's," says Molina.

"Sounds about right," says Tibedoe. "We'll brief the chief when you finish and get back to the office, and we'll see where we go from here." He hangs up the phone. "With Tony's identification of the two dead guys, there appears to be a link back to Boston," he says to Officer Youngblood. "Tony's wrapping things up at the coroner's office and will be back in the office in about an hour. I'll brief the chief in on our current status of the case and see what, if anything, he wants us to do."

"You mean he might tell us to stop investigating...just stop?" asks Youngblood.

"Well, Tina, the case appears to be that of justifiable homicide. I mean, I'm sure he'll want me to talk it over with the district attorney, but O'Connor was in his total rights to defend himself inside his own home. I can't see where O'Connor did anything wrong," says Tibedoe.

"Don't you think he could be in danger?" asks Youngblood.

"Yes I do, Tina, and I think O'Connor knows that too. He's more than capable of handling himself, and I have no doubt he'll seek out those responsible."

CHAPTER 4
HANK'S PLACE

LIAM LEAVES HIS CONDO, taking Sandy with him. He lifts Sandy up and places her into the back seat of his 1979 Toyota Land Cruiser wagon, a vehicle bought new by his father and kept in Liam's possession since his death in 2012. Liam removes the back floor panel and retrieves a Glock .40 caliber semi-automatic handgun and several sixteen-round magazines from a hidden compartment underneath the back seat.

"Sandy, it's back to work for us, old girl! Let's go see Henry," says Liam.

He places the gun and magazines in the glove box and calls Sandy to sit up front in the passenger seat.

"Okay, Sandy, let's go," says Liam.

They travel to a storage facility in downtown Port Saint Lucie called Hank Swank's Storage Rentals. They stop at the office, and Liam lets Sandy out of the passenger side.

"That's one butt-ugly vehicle you got there, Liam," says Henry, who meets them at the front door of the office. "I see you brought Sandy with you today!" Sandy begins to growl at Henry. "Are you here on business or just a family visit?" asks Henry.

"No, sir," says Liam, "I'm here to pick up some files from my storage unit."

"I talked to your mother earlier in the day. She told me you had some visitors at your place last night. I guess everything worked out fine, but she's pretty worried."

"Uncle Henry, I need to find out why someone would want me dead. Until I do, being here puts you all in danger, and I can't have that. Henry, I'm going to my unit to get some things. It would be best if you stayed here," says Liam.

"Please take Sandy with you. She just sits and growls at me. I just don't understand, after all these years. You'd think we'd be friends by now," says Henry.

"Well, Henry, that dog is a good judge of character. Or in your case, lack of character," laughs Liam.

"Get up here, Sandy," he says as he opens the front passenger door.

"Henry, you're right. The Cruiser is an ugly tank, but she gets me around. And besides, this old wagon and I have shared a lot of fond memories," says Liam.

Liam and Sandy drive through the storage facility and finally reach his unit, which is located on the second floor. He obtained this unit from his Uncle Henry after the death of Kelley. He uses the unit as a sanctuary of sorts, a refuge to see and feel items of Kelley's. This somehow soothes his pain. Liam has been to the unit every week since his arrival in Port Saint Lucie, and with every visit he leaves in tears.

"Okay, Sandy, this is it! Let's go, girl," says Liam.

Sandy jumps down from the Cruiser and gets into the elevator with Liam. The elevator stops on the second floor, and Sandy and Liam start to walk toward the storage unit.

"Sandy, this is a business trip. I promise no tears this time," says Liam.

Yet when he opens the door and starts to look at Kelley's personal belongings, her clothes, her favorite furniture, and smells the perfume off her clothes, he begins to tear up. He looks over at Sandy and notices she is staring at him.

"What...?" he says, looking at Sandy. "It's this damn medication I'm taking."

He makes his way to an area where there are several file cabinets. He opens the cabinets and begins to look through copies of his past investigations. Copies of complete investigations dating back to his first assigned case as a detective. Liam looks through several homicide cases, murder books, and locates a past homicide case that interests him.

"This is what I'm looking for. The Lonnie Jackson homicide," says Liam, looking at Sandy.

He takes the homicide murder book and places it on top of a gun safe. He continues to look through a second file cabinet, but stops and shakes his head and says, "I never had a case involving a Shea, I don't think."

Liam continues looking through old investigations for the next forty-five minutes or so. He slams the file cabinet shut and goes to the gun safe, opens it, and removes .40 caliber ammunition, a Winchester 12-gauge 870short-barreled pump shotgun, and two boxes of 12-gauge ammo.

"Come on, Sandy, time to go," says Liam. He and Sandy leave the storage unit and return back to the Cruiser. Liam thinks to himself, Dad sure knew what he was doing when he built this hidden compartment area under the back seat. He places the handgun, shotgun, and ammunition in the compartment and replaces the backseat.

"Okay, old girl, let's go," says Liam. Sandy jumps in the front seat, and they drive back toward the front office.

Henry meets Liam at the exit and asks, "Did you find what you're looking for?"

He looks into Liam's eyes and says, "You're going back into the jungle, aren't you?"

"Henry, this time the animals came here. I've got to go. I won't put what family I have left in danger," says Liam, looking at Henry.

"You go do what you need to, son, but you come back. I can't deal with your mother alone. Since we were kids, she's been one stubborn Irish woman," says Henry.

Liam notices the front sign to the business, and while chuckling says, "Hey, with a name like Hank Swank, you can handle anything."

"Now, you know this place was already named Swank's Storage when I bought it. I thought it was a catchy business name, so I just added Hank to the sign," replies Henry.

"Well, Henry O'Hara, I've got to go. I'd be obliged if you'd look in on Mama while I'm away," says Liam. He looks at Henry and wants to say more, but Henry looks at him and says,

"Do what you have to, but come back to us!"

Liam and Sandy drive off.

⌒◦⌒

The door opens from Chief Green's office at the Port Saint Lucie Police Department and Detective Tibedoe asks loudly, "Tony, Officer Youngblood, will you join me in the chief's office, please?"

Molina, having just returned from the Coroner's Office, gathers some papers together, expecting to brief the chief on the autopsy and the identification of the John Does. Officer Youngblood is somewhat surprised to be called into the chief's office and gets nervous.

They enter the office, and Chief Green says, "I've called you all in after talking with John about the status of the investigation. John has given me the updates as to who the two dead guys are, and their criminal background. John and I have spoken with the district attorney's office, and we are all in agreement that this shooting was a case of justifiable homicide. No crime was committed by O'Connor. With that in mind, your investigation is completed. Now, having said that, John and I believe that O'Connor's life is still in danger. John, you and Tony go and speak to O'Connor and let him know what the DA's decision on this matter was. I'm sure he'll be glad to hear the news. Also, let him know that a two-man patrol vehicle will be outside his condo for the next several days or so. What I've learned about Liam O'Connor is that he's going hunting, and probably won't be around long. I also wanted to tell all of you, you all did a fine job out there. I know this was Officer Youngblood's first time assisting in a homicide investigation."

Chief Green looks at Officer Youngblood and says, "I believe you have good instincts as an investigator. I think when a spot opens up in the detective division, you should put in a transfer request. Tony, you were right! Shea was in the Army, those were military tats on his arm. Doc Hill found positive identification through Shea's military records. Good work," says Chief Green.

"Chief, Tony and I will go and speak with O'Connor," says Tibedoe.

"Okay, take Youngblood with you, too," says Chief Green.

The detectives leave the chief's office and meet outside in the parking lot of the police station.

"Detective Molina and Officer Youngblood, there is one last thing I wanted to talk to you about, away from the chief," says Tibedoe. "If I can figure out that something is going on with you two, you can bet the chief knows it, too." You two need to get your shit together fast! Don't say anything. This is where I talk, and you listen. Both the chief and I see eye to eye when it comes to workplace romance. It usually ends badly. My suggestion to you two is, get over it. If you don't, your careers could be affected, and you both have bright futures here. You think about what I'm saying. You could be working together for many years to come, possibly as partners. Can you deal with that?" asks Tibedoe.

"This ends my fatherly advice for today. Now, let's go talk with Mr. O'Connor."

The three drive to O'Connor's condo, saying nothing on the ride over.

Liam and Sandy arrive back at the condo, and he begins to pack for Boston. He wonders what he will do with Sandy on this trip. He doesn't want to take her, because he knows he might not be returning home. He remembers to bring his favorite leather jacket, an old black jacket given to him some twenty-five years ago by Kelley. He recalls Kelley telling him,

"Liam, if you want to be properly warmed, you come home. But until that happens, this jacket will have to do the job."

Liam wore the jacket in the Boston winters, but always looked forward to coming home.

Sandy begins to bark and starts to pace near the front door. Liam knows someone is outside the home. He places his gun under his jacket and starts toward the door when he hears a knock. Liam approaches the door slowly, looks out the front window and sees Lieutenant Tibedoe, Molina and Officer Youngblood. He places the gun and jacket on the kitchen counter and opens the front door.

"Mr. O'Connor, we have some news for you. May we please come in?" asks Lieutenant Tibedoe.

"Sure," says Liam. He looks back at his jacket on the kitchen table, sees the gun is completely covered, and continues to open the door. Tibedoe, Molina, and Youngblood enter the residence and sit down in the living room.

"Liam, the chief and I ran this case by the district attorney. The DA believes this is justifiable homicide and not a crime," says Tibedoe. "So as far as we're concerned, this investigation is closed. We just wanted to let you know this."

"Well, thank you for coming by and telling me. Were you able to identify my two visitors last night?" asks Liam.

"Yes, the light complexioned guy was identified as Bobby Dale Pentacost, and the other we identified as Daniel Scott Shea," says Lieutenant Tibedoe.

Detective Molina asks, "Do you recognize any of those names, maybe from past cases or something?" Detective Molina, Tibedoe and Officer Youngblood look at Liam.

Liam looks into Detective Molina's eyes and says, "I don't recall those names." He realizes that his left hand is slightly shaking uncontrollably and puts the hand in his pants pocket. Officer Youngblood looks around the condo and notices a red canvas bag with the logo "Boston College Eagles" on it, placed near the kitchen counter, and sees the jacket near the bag. She continues to scan the room. "Is there something I can help you with, Officer?" asks Liam as he notices her looking around the residence.

"No, Mr. O'Connor, I was looking just for Sandy."

"Sandy is probably lying in her favorite chair in my office," says Liam. "This is

63

the time of day she usually takes her nap."

"Sounds like my kinda dog," says Officer Youngblood.

"Well, I was wondering if I could ask a big favor of you, Officer Youngblood," says Liam.

He looks at Officer Youngblood, Detective Molina, and Lieutenant Tibedoe and walks toward Officer Youngblood, getting a couple of feet from her. As Liam walks towards Youngblood, Molina becomes unsettled and starts toward Liam.

He looks over at Detective Molina and says, "Easy, Skippy, I'm on your side." Liam looks down at her face and asks, "Officer?"

"Please call me Tina," requests Officer Youngblood.

"Okay then. Tina, would you mind looking after Sandy for a few days while I'm gone?"

Lieutenant Tibedoe asks, "Liam, where are you headed to?"

"I'm driving back to Boston for a few days to see some family. I should only be gone for about five days or so. I would really appreciate it. Sandy doesn't get along well with most people, but she didn't mind being with you last night," says Liam. "I can't take her to my mama's place. If you can't watch her or don't have the room for her, I understand. Dogs aren't for everyone," says Liam. He looks into the eyes of Tina and flashes back to a time when he looked into the eyes of Kelley, remembering her green eyes, soft pale skin and her long, flowing auburn hair. He starts to lean down as though he is going to smell Kelley's hair, but he stops, realizing it's Tina in front of him.

Tina steps closer to Liam while he stares into her eyes. She starts to breathe faster, feeling a warm, tingling sensation on the back of her neck. She reaches back to rub her neck and thinks to herself: compose yourself. Breathe through your nose. After a long, awkward pause, he looks toward the others as though what just happened surprised him. What seemed like a frozen moment in time was really no more than a few seconds of direct eye contact.

Liam steps back a few paces and notices his hand has stopped shaking. He says to Tina, "Well, hmm, if you can't..."

"I would be glad to watch her," says Tina. "I'll be here to pick her up after I complete my shift in a few hours."

"Very good, then," says Liam. "I'll have everything ready and waiting for you."

"Okay, Liam, we just came to give the latest information from the district attorney," says Lieutenant Tibedoe. Detective Molina, Tibedoe, and Officer Youngblood begin walking toward the front door when Sandy comes from the office and walks toward Officer Youngblood. Youngblood reaches down and starts petting Sandy.

"Tibedoe," says Liam, "last night my handgun was seized. What are the chances I can get it back today, since I committed no crime?"

"Not happening today, Liam," says Lieutenant Tibedoe. "Guns are released back to the owners when the Department of Justice clears them, which can take several weeks, as you know."

"I thought so," says Liam.

Lieutenant Tibedoe, Molina, and Officer Youngblood leave Liam's place and return to their vehicle.

"Sir," asks Officer Youngblood, "are you still going to have officers assigned to O'Connor until he leaves?"

"Tina, it's done. Look over there," says Tibedoe.

She looks over to the parking lot area of the complex and sees a marked patrol vehicle with two uniformed officers.

"They have been told to shadow him until otherwise directed. This protection detail will continue until the chief shuts it down," says Detective Tibedoe.

"It makes it difficult to do much, being watched like that," says Molina with a smile.

"So you're going to watch his dog?" asks Tibedoe.

"Tina, you be careful. When you are with him, you too are in danger. You may be blinded to that right now," says Tibedoe.

"Tina, John is right. I saw how you looked at him in there. We may have had our time, and I wish it would have lasted, but like so many of my relationships, it didn't. Oh hell, I know I have, let's say, relationship issues with women, but the way I saw you look at him was the way I want a woman to feel with me. Just don't expect too much from him," says Molina.

"I mean, when he's looking at you, who is he *really* seeing?" asks Tibedoe.

"That dude has issues, but who doesn't?" says Tony. "I just don't want to see you get hurt." Detective Molina, Lieutenant Tibedoe, and Officer Youngblood get into their vehicle, and Detective Tibedoe turns to Tony and says,

"I guess if you peel an onion a layer at a time, you might be surprised what you'll find."

"Yeah, that's true with all of us," says Tina. They drive away with Lieutenant Tibedoe realizing that Molina and Youngblood are going to be all right.

Liam looks out his window and sees the detectives drive off, and spots the marked patrol vehicle in the parking lot outside his condo. He continues to load his bags into his vehicle. He checks the engine's oil level and other fluids, like his dad had taught him. With a twenty-four hour drive ahead of him, he needs the Toyota

Cruiser to be reliable. I have no doubt the Cruiser will hold up, but will I, wonders Liam as he looks at the Cruiser. I'm taking pills just to make myself stop shaking. I haven't had a drink of Jameson for over ten months, and yet I see, smell, and talk to Kelley like she's alive.

He thinks back about eight months ago, when his doctor told him he had Parkinson's. He knows, in time, what can become of him. His mind and body could weaken, and he'll become challenged by life's simple tasks. He laughs. That's my damn Irish luck. I survive over thirty years as a cop, and my body turns on itself, thinks Liam.

The challenges ahead of him bring renewed energy to Liam. He continues to pack the Cruiser with the proper food and drink for the journey back to Boston. Beef jerky, Gatorade, and a Starbucks card will be a good start. He checks the computer for the road and weather conditions from Port Saint Lucie to Boston, Massachusetts. Nothing could be finer than Boston in the winter, thinks Liam. He notices Sandy walk to the front door as though someone is approaching. He retrieves his handgun from the kitchen counter and walks toward the front door. He looks outside an adjoining window and sees that it's Officer Youngblood. He opens the door before she can knock, which catches her by surprise. With his handgun tucked behind his back leg, Liam continues to open the door and says,

"Please come on in."

Tina looks down at Liam's right arm and spots that he has tucked a handgun toward his backside.

"I see you found another gun, Liam," she says.

"Sorry about that. Hell of a way to greet a lady," says Liam while backing up and lifting the gun out in plain view. "Let me put this thing down." He moves over to the kitchen counter and places the handgun back on the counter near his jacket.

"Please come in. I don't always meet people at the door with a gun in my hand, but stuff happens with me," says Liam.

"That's okay. I'm armed too," says Tina.

Liam notices that she's not in uniform. In fact, she's wearing jeans and a tee shirt that reads USMC Explosive Ordinance

Disposal School, Camp Pendleton, California. He also sees she has a gun tucked in her waistband underneath her shirt. Liam does another once-over of Tina and thinks to himself, damned attractive, but she can't be but a few years older than my daughter.

"I really appreciate your willingness to watch Sandy. I know earlier it may have been difficult for you to say no to my request, but if you've changed your mind, it's really okay. I can just board her for a few days," says Liam.

"No," says Tina, "I'm looking forward to this. She seems like a great dog."

"Please sit down, let me move my bags from the chair. Please sit," says Liam as he points to an empty chair. "She really is. She's a good listener, too. She and I have had some good conversations over the past several months or so." Sandy comes to the side of Liam and sits beside him. He strokes her head while looking at her. "She means a lot to me," he says. "I was thinking about this before you came over. It might be easier for you to stay here and dog sit... I mean, I know you work. You could stay here, or just come and go. It might be easier for both you and Sandy. I know this sounds forward of me, but I plan on hitting the road, so the place would be yours.

"I would like that," says Tina.

"Good. You might tell Tibedoe that the babysitters won't be needed anymore," says Liam.

He looks at Sandy and at Tina, and says, "Nice shirt," staring at her chest.

Tina's chest is that of a well-developed woman, but he's referring to the print on the shirt. However, Liam thinks what he just said could have been taken a different way. "I didn't mean it that way," says Liam as his hands reach out into two curved simulated breasts. He looks at his hands and just shakes his head.

"I'm really not a pervert. Forgive my manners."

"That's okay, my husband used to do the same thing. I haven't had such a sweet compliment in years," says Tina.

"I didn't know you were married. I just assumed...I mean, you and Detective Molina seemed like you had a thing going. I just thought..."

"My husband was killed in Iraq about five years ago. This is actually his shirt," says Tina. "He was an EOD specialist."

"I'm sorry to hear that," says Liam.

"We were married for a year when he got deployed. No kids. God had a different plan, I guess," says Tina.

"Yeah, I know about changes of plans. Personally, I think it sucks. I'm not much into change at my age," says Liam. "My mother says that very same thing about change, that God has a different plan. I guess it will happen whether I want it to or not," says Liam.

"I saw a picture of your wife and daughter while I was searching your bedroom last night. They're beautiful women," says Tina.

"Molley and Kelley look a lot alike. They too, are gifted in the chest area," says Liam with a smile. "My wife used to say, 'Liam, my lollies'—that's what she called her boobs—'are working themselves down South the older I get.' I would tell her, where they go, I go!" he says. "She would just point her finger at me and say, "Liam Matthew O'Connor. You know better. But I love you anyway."

Liam looks at the photograph and remembers the time it was taken, and smiles.

"Your daughter is lovely too. She works out of Atlanta, right?" asks Tina.

He looks at his daughter in the photograph and says, "Yes, she lives in Atlanta and works at a big hospital as their human resource manager. We're not on speaking terms right now. She blames me for Kelley's death, and I'm not sure she's wrong."

Tina looks at Liam, and he stares back for several seconds. She wants to say something but feels it's inappropriate.

"All right, Tina, I need to hit the road. Do you have a cell phone number I can call, so I can check up on Sandy from time to time?" asks Liam. Tina gives Liam her cell phone number, and he starts to gather his last bags from his home.

"Do you have a cell number you can be reached at, in case I need to get a hold of you?" asks Tina.

"No, Tina, I think it's best I call you from pay phones," says Liam.

He works his way toward the front door, stops and looks down at Sandy. "Sandy, you be good. I'll be back soon." He looks at Tina and says, "And if I don't make it back, God has a plan. We just need to accept it. Now I must tell you, Sandy is a great conversationalist. She says a lot with her eyes."

Liam looks at Tina saying nothing as he turns and leaves the condo, walking slowly toward the Cruiser.

Tina watches as Liam gets into the old Cruiser and drives off. She shuts the door and turns to Sandy and says, "Your eyes aren't the only ones talking. I can't seem to catch my breath when that man is around."

CHAPTER 5

PLEASE COME TO BOSTON

LIAM DRIVES AWAY FROM THE CONDO headed toward Interstate 95, northbound to Boston. He looks at the passenger seat and sees several past murder books that he has retrieved from his storage unit at Hank Swank's. He looks down at his watch and sees it indicates eight o'clock at night. He predicts he'll be in Boston the following day by six p.m., or close to it. He opens the murder book of Lonnie Jackson. The first page is a crime and incident face page written by him. He looks at the date of the investigation, June 1990, and sees the name Detective Gordon Zimmer. Liam closes the murder book and continues to drive. He recalls the first time he met Detective Gordon Zimmer...

"Come in," says Lieutenant Mahoney. "It's nice to have you in Homicide. I've heard good things about you and your time in the Sexual Assault and Abuse Investigation Unit. I pulled your file and was impressed with your street patrol experience."

"Thank you, sir," says Liam.

Liam enters the office and sits in a single chair positioned directly across the desk from Lt. Mahoney. "Did you know Liam, your father and I worked the streets together for many years?"

"Yes, sir. He told me how you two Southies had some run-ins with the Irish and Italian mobsters from time to time, back in the day," says Liam.

"Your father has quite a reputation on the streets. He's one tough Irishman," says Lt. Mahoney.

"I fear no other man, sir!" says Liam, laughing. "Lt. Mahoney, he told me you held your own out there as well."

"Yeah, but Joseph and I were able to move around the docks and other places freely because of Joseph's relationship with Francis Salvador Pennilli," says Lt. Mahoney.

"Uncle Pennilli and my father were friends as kids, and then they also served in Korea together. To this day, I call him my uncle, even though I know he's not," says Liam.

"Sal and his father had a lot of pull on the streets back then. Maybe even more so now," says Lt. Mahoney. "Liam, I saw you play against Army in '77," says Lt. Mahoney.

"Well, sir, we were up big, so I got in for a quarter or so," says Liam.

"Your old man loved to watch you play. He talked my ear off about you being at Boston College. I heard you got hurt in the U-Mass game," says Lt. Mahoney.

"Yes sir, that ended my football career," says Liam.

"Well, enough bullshitting, Liam. I'm partnering you up with Zim... Gordon Zimmer. His friends call him Zim for short, but you should call him by his first name until he tells you otherwise. Do you know Zimmer?" asks Lt. Mahoney.

"I've heard of him," replies Liam.

"I bet you have," laughs the lieutenant. "Here's what I expect from you. Zim has worked thirty-two years in this department and has one year left before he plans on retiring.

He's had a long and distinguished career, and I want to see him finish," says Lt. Mahoney. "But what I need you to know is that Zim likes to drink. He has a limited vocabulary, and hates most people, especially the brass in this department. His ability to investigate homicides and to testify in court now concern me," says Lt. Mahoney. "Now, having said that, you can learn a few things from him, if he likes you. I want you and him out of the office by eight-fifteen in the morning, and don't return back to the office until quarter till five. You do all the driving. You get called out at night, you do the driving. You pull a case, you write the paper, and if at all possible, you do all the testifying in court. Zim doesn't know it, but he's retired. Now, is this fair to you? No, and I don't give a damn. I picked you for this unit because you're smart, you know the streets and can navigate your way within this department. That's the deal. Take it or leave it. What will it be?"

"I'm in, sir," says Liam.

"Okay, then open the door behind you, Liam," states Lt. Mahoney.

Liam opens the door, and Lt. Mahoney yells out, "Zim, get your sorry ass in here."

Gordon Zimmer walks toward the door as Liam looks and sees a thin, gray-haired man wearing black framed glasses and a sixties-style black suit walking toward the office. Liam notices several mustard stains on his jacket and white dress shirt.

"Zim, I'd like you to meet your new partner, Liam O'Connor." Liam puts his hand out for a handshake. Zim reaches out and shakes his hand.

"Lieutenant, are you giving me my very own lucky charm?" asks Zim.

"Zim, I've already talked with Liam about what I expect from him. What I expect from you is your best effort at work, and from what I'm seeing, you're not doing so good. You look like shit and smell like whiskey," says Lt. Mahoney. "Go to the Goodwill and get some new suits. Suits with color, suits with style, suits from this decade. You two get the hell out of my office."

Zim and Liam leave the office and walk toward the homicide desks of the detective division. Zim turns to Liam and says,

"My desk is near the window. From here I can see all the ladies coming and going. You'd be surprised what I see, with or without the binoculars. Take the desk across from mine. It's not prime territory, but you won't be here that long. I bet you're gone in less than a month."

Liam looks at Zim and says nothing. He looks at Zim's desk and sees a daily calendar that features a Boston Red Sox fact of the day. Liam sees he's a Red Sox fan. He spots a photograph of Zim and Lieutenant Mahoney inside Alumni Stadium of Boston College.

Liam begins moving items from his desk in Sex Crimes to Homicide. A clerk from Crime Reports stops in front of Liam's and Zimmer's desk and asks if this is his new assignment.

"Julie Santora, let me introduce you to my partner, Gordon Zimmer," says Liam.

Julie turns to Zimmer and says, "Nice to meet you, sir."

While all the time she's staring at his suit, flattop haircut, and mustard-stained white shirt. Liam smiles and watches as lovely Julie walks away.

"O'Connor," says Zim, "you might last longer than a month. You don't talk much, do you?"

"Quiet people have the loudest minds," says Liam with a grin.

Liam continues to place all of his belongings from his desk in the Sexual Assault and Abuse Investigations Unit, to his new desk in Homicide. His partner, Detective Gordon Zimmer, sits at his desk just looking at Liam. He wants to ask Liam the Red Sox fact of the day.

"Liam, let me test your baseball knowledge with the Red Sox trivia question of the day."

"Okay, Zim, fire away. Baseball is not my main sport, but I'll give it a shot," says Liam.

"Okay, here we go. Let's make this interesting. If you get the answer right, lunch is on me today. If you get it wrong, you buy lunch."

"Deal. Fire away," says Liam.

"Carl Yastrzemski leads most every Red Sox offense category except triples and homeruns. Who leads in all-time homeruns?"

Liam just smiles, because his dad's favorite baseball player was Ted Williams. He knows the answer to Zim's question is Ted Williams, but having looked at his mustard-stained shirt and the grease stains on his jacket, he thinks Zim's likely in need of a free meal more than him. Besides, since it's his first day working with Zim, it's only right to pay some dues. He delays his answer for a few seconds, and then tells Zim, "It's Jimmie Foxx."

"Wrong, sir. The Red Sox fact of the day is that it was actually Ted Williams who leads in all-time homeruns. Sweet, lunch is on Liam. I feel my luck a'changing. Who knows, maybe you are my lucky charm," says Zim with a shit-eating grin on his face.

"Zim, O'Connor, get your sorry asses in my office now," yells Lieutenant Mahoney from his office.

What now? wonders Liam.

"Second time in one day I'm being called to the lieutenant's office. What the hell did you do now?" asks Zim.

Liam and Zim walk back from their desk toward the lieutenant's office, and all the time Liam's thinking, I should have gotten Zim out of the office.

"Sit your asses down." Both men sit as ordered. "Zim, Liam, I need you to go see the on-duty desk sergeant downstairs, Sgt. Perez. He has a lady at his desk who wants us to check on her ex-husband. She believes he's killed his current girlfriend and may have committed suicide."

"Lieutenant," says Zim, "can't you send the kid? I mean, I'm always getting these crackpots coming to the station, wanting to tell me outrageous shit, sir."

"Liam, take that partner of yours out of here and check this out," replies the lieutenant as he stares and shakes his head at Zim.

Liam and Zim get up from their chairs and walk out of the lieutenant's office, and start to walk downstairs. Zim looks over at Liam and says, "Lucky charm, my ass!"

"Hey Zim, I guess that lunch will just have to wait. Tough break," laughs Liam.

Liam and Zim meet Sgt. Perez at the front desk.

"Sarge, how can we help you out?" asks Liam.

Sgt. Perez points to a Hispanic lady and two kids seated on the bench in the waiting room. He says, "The lady believes her ex-husband killed his current girlfriend."

Zim asks, "Does she speak English? Because I don't speak Spanish."

"That's okay, Zim. I speak Spanish, if that's a problem," says Liam.

Sgt. Perez just laughs and says, "She speaks English, so maybe Zim shouldn't talk to her."

Zim and Liam introduce themselves to the lady and ask if she would like to step into a side office where it's private. Liam asks if she would like something to drink, or maybe something for her four- and six-year-old children. Mrs. Angelica Hernandez tells Zim and Liam,

"Thank you, my children and I are fine for now."

"Ma'am, the front desk sergeant said you came in here today concerned about your ex-husband," says Liam.

Mrs. Hernandez tells Liam and Zim that she got a call from her ex-husband last night, at about 9 o'clock in the evening. She says that she and her ex, Jesus Hernandez, also known as "Chuy," have been divorced for the last year. He pays child support and has been coming by to see the kids every week. Mrs. Hernandez tells Liam, as Zim looks on, that Chuy called last night and told her he wasn't going to be able to see the kids for a while. He said he's done something stupid, and to tell the kids that he loves them. She says he sounded strange and told her she was his only true love. She asked him what was going on. He told her he got into an argument with Irma, but wouldn't tell her anymore. She says early this morning, around 6 a.m., he called her again and told her he had killed Irma, his girlfriend, and he was going to kill himself. She tried calling him back several times, but got no answer. Mrs. Hernandez says that's when she came to the police station.

"Ma'am, where does your ex-husband live?" asks Liam.

"He lives in the projects on Lenox Street in the South End. He lives in apartment 210, with his girlfriend and his sister."

"Does Chuy own a gun?" asks Liam.

Mrs. Hernandez says, "I don't think so. He works in construction, he has so many tools and stuff. I don't believe he has a gun. I mean, he's never been in any trouble. He's always been a good provider for me and the kids."

"Okay, ma'am. We're going to drive over to the projects and see if we can locate Chuy. We'll just see what's going on, if anything," says Liam.

Liam and Zim escort the children and Mrs. Hernandez back out to the front desk area. Zim asks Sgt. Perez if he could have a patrol unit drive Mrs. Hernandez home, as she came to the station by bus. He tells Sgt. Perez,

"Please let us know if she calls and speaks to her ex-husband from the station. Liam and I will be en route to check on this guy's welfare."

Liam and Zim walk out to the parking lot and locate their unmarked detective vehicle. Zim starts toward the driver's side, and Liam says, "Can't have that Zim, I'm under orders to drive."

Zim looks at Liam and shakes his head. "My own driver, too! I'm getting my lunch paid for, I'm being driven around like I'm brass or something, and I have my own lucky charm...Let's eat, I'm starved," he gripes.

"Gordon," says Liam.

"Kid, it's Zim to you! No one, I mean no one, calls me Gordon," says Zim.

"We're going to check this out now. It's probably nothing. If so, it's lunch time," says Liam.

The two drive across town to the South End and locate the projects on Lenox Street. Zim and Liam walk upstairs to apartment 210 and approach the front door. A man opens the front door and steps out, just before Liam and Zim can reach the door. He looks at the two detectives and seems surprised. Liam asks the man,

"Sir, is your name Jesus or 'Chuy' Hernandez?"

He looks at the two detectives and says, "Yeah, who are you?"

"We are Detectives Zimmer and O'Connor of the Boston Police."

"What do you guys want?" asks Chuy.

"Well, your ex-wife, Angelica, sent us over here. She was pretty worried about you, and so were your kids," responds Liam.

"Do you mind if we come in and talk to you for a little bit?"

Chuy replies, "No, it's okay. Come in."

Chuy, Zim, and Liam walk back into the apartment and are asked to sit down at the table.

Zim asks, "Is everything okay with you and Irma?"

Chuy starts to cry. Liam asks, "Chuy, would you mind if I look around the apartment?"

Chuy says, "No, I don't mind. I'm the only one here. My sister and her kids left yesterday and are staying at her boyfriend's apartment."

Zim asks, "Where's Irma?"

Chuy again says nothing and just looks at Zim. Liam starts looking through the apartment. He asks, "Do you have your own room, or where do you sleep?"

Chuy points to his room and says, "That's my room. My sister and her kids stay in the other room, down the hall."

Liam sees the apartment has two bedrooms, a center hallway, and a kitchen just off the living room. The front door opens up into the living room.

Liam confirms the first bedroom down the hallway is Chuy's room. He opens the closed door to the bedroom and walks in. He sees a large pool of blood on the carpet floor next to the bed. Liam also sees there are dozens of hand tools, power saws, and a large compressor in the room as well. He looks down at the pooled blood and sees a carpenter's belt with a hammer and a single 9 millimeter shell casing resting in the pouch full of 16d nails. The belt also holds a tape measure, carpenter's pencil and level. Liam looks at the wall and can see a hole about the size of a 9mm bullet, along with blood spatter. Liam continues to look through the room. He sees a photo of Chuy's wife, Angelica, and their two children next to the bed. The picture frame has been broken and the glass shattered. There is blood on the front of the picture, and what Liam believes is brain matter on the wall. Liam continues to look through the room.

He notes, near the closet, a caulking gun with white caulking compound loaded in the gun. Liam walks down the hallway and finds the door to the second bedroom closed and locked.

"Chuy," asks Liam, "is this bedroom your sister's?"

"Yeah. She's gone, so she always locks it when she leaves."

Liam doesn't enter the room, but continues on with his search, now heading toward the kitchen. After searching the kitchen, he walks over to where Zim and Chuy are seated. Zim looks at Liam and says, "He won't say anything when I ask him about Irma."

Liam asks Chuy to stand up. He stands up, and Liam says, "You're under arrest for murder."

Liam then places the handcuffs on him.

Chuy turns to Zim and Liam, and starts to cry.

"Okay, I'll tell you everything," he says.

Liam tells Zim that he'll have to get a telephonic search warrant for the apartment.

"To cover our asses, Zim, I'll just get a warrant before I see what's in the locked bedroom."

Zim suggests he take Jesus Hernandez down to the station and speak to him about Irma.

"We'll have a nice little chat, won't we, Chuy?" says Zim.

Zim takes Chuy from the apartment and walks him downstairs while Liam contacts the on-duty judge by telephone and requests permission to search the entire residence. Detective Gordon Zimmer drives Chuy to the headquarters and places him in a locked and secured interview room. He leaves Hernandez there alone, crying.

Liam is granted a search warrant from the on-duty judge, which now allows him to search the entire apartment and its contents. Liam forces open the back bedroom door to the sister's room, expecting to find a dead body. He searches the room, closet, and adjoining bathroom, but finds no body or evidence of a crime. Liam goes back to Chuy's bedroom and once again begins to search. He finds, hidden underneath the top mattress and the box spring, a Ruger semi-automatic, 9mm caliber handgun. The gun is loaded with six additional rounds in the magazine. He doesn't locate a body. Liam searches for a crawl space, but finds none. He walks out into the living room and sits down on the couch. He wonders if each of these apartments have a small storage unit outside. He looks through the kitchen again, but locates no additional items of evidence. He sits in the living room and looks back at the bathroom. He walks down and re-checks the bathroom, but finds no blood in the sink or bathtub.

Liam walks from the bathroom toward the living room, when he notices a piece of black plastic beneath the couch. As he walks towards the couch, he sees the plastic sticking out the sides of the skirting of the upholstered couch. He reaches under the couch and lifts it up. He discovers two large black construction-size plastic bags. The two bags are about 6 feet in length, and are wrapped around something that is about 5 to 6 feet in length. Liam notices that the second black plastic bag is wrapped over the open end of the first bag. The objects inside are completely wrapped in plastic, securely kept in place by gray duct tape.

The tape is wrapped almost around the entire length of the objects. Liam moves the couch to the side and lays out the plastic bags. He suspects what's in the bag is the body of Jesus Hernandez's girlfriend, Irma. As Liam moves the bags, he can feel the physical shape of a human body. He removes one of the bags that covers the head of the body. He discovers it's indeed the body of Irma. Liam sees that Irma had white makeup applied to her face, along with bright red lipstick placed on her lips. This make-up has been put on postmortem, after death. As he looks closer, he sees white caulking compound to the left temple, and then again just above the right eye-socket. This appears to be the location the bullet entered and exited from the head. He looks closer and sees a small amount of blood seepage from both wounds. Liam thinks to himself, nice job on the caulking. The makeup and the color of the caulking matches perfectly. Liam realizes, I should stop processing. He calls the evidence technicians and the coroner's office. The evidence technicians and coroner's personnel will assist in processing the crime scene for additional evidence. He stops, calls Zimmer and lets him know what he has found. Zim tells Liam that he is about to start the taped interview with Hernandez.

Four hours later, Liam finishes processing the apartment. Irma Negrette Soto was identified by coroner's personnel as the deceased. She was taken to the morgue for further examination. Liam is driven back to headquarters and meets up with Zim, back at their desks in the Homicide Unit.

"I'm starved, kid. Let's gets some lunch... oh, that's right, lunch is on you today. Let's go, I know a good steak place in Brighton!" says Zim.

Liam replies, "What happened, Zim? What did the guy say?"

"Oh!, Chuy confessed to the whole thing," replies Zim.

Liam and Zim walk out of the police headquarters and get into their vehicle. Liam drives to Brighton as Zim explains what Chuy confessed to. Zim says,

"That guy was primed to confess. I maybe asked him six or seven questions after I advised him of his rights. Chuy said he and his girlfriend, Irma Soto, had been listening to some music in his bedroom and were about ready to have sex. He said Irma didn't like the picture of Chuy's ex-wife and children above the headboard of the bed. She told Chuy to remove the photo from the wall because it 'killed' the moment for her. Chuy said he was taking the photo down when Irma said, 'How could you have ever been married to that fat bitch?' He said that made him angry because she was talking down to the mother of his children. He said he struck her with the picture over the head one time. Chuy said Irma just laughed at him, because the picture had broken when he hit her in the head. He reached over to the nightstand and grabbed his 9 mm Ruger and shot Irma, one time, in the left side of her head. Her brains were blown all over the walls. He said, 'First I just sat there for a while thinking someone might have heard the shot, but because we had the music up loud, no one came to the door to check on the shot.' Chuy said, 'I got kind of got scared after I shot her! She started bleeding from her head, making a mess on the carpet. I thought I'd be able to stop the bleeding if I just put some caulking compound in the holes in her head. I mean, after I put the caulking compound in the holes, she stopped bleeding. Then I noticed her face had some burn marks on it, so I decided to put some makeup on her. My sister had some white stuff you put on your face in her bathroom. I decided to just put it on her face, along with some lipstick, too.'"

Zim said Chuy slept with her that night in the same room. He said he got scared and didn't know what to do with the body, so he put her in some construction-grade plastic 50-gallon bags and stuffed her up under the couch in the morning. He was going to leave and go to Mexico when we came walking down the hallway. Zim asked Chuy why he didn't just leave her there the night before. Why did he sleep with her all night? He said he was aroused by her dead body! He said, 'She was much easier to deal with.' Zimmer said that Chuy had sex with Irma's corpse several times through the night, until he shoved her up underneath the couch in the morning.

Liam and Zimmer arrive at the steakhouse, and Zim turns to Liam and says,

"Let's eat, I'm starved."

The two enter the restaurant and have a late lunch before heading back to the office. Zimmer and Liam walk back into the Homicide office and start toward their desks. Zim looks down at his desk and sees a caulking gun with a note next to it that reads: "Presented to Detectives G. Zimmer and L. O'Connor for outstanding detective work on 'The Night Caulker Case'." Liam looks to his desk and sees a small jar of cherries with a note that reads: "You'll always remember your first homicide!"

Liam sits at his desk writing reports for the next few hours, all the time listening to Zimmer strut around the detective division, talking about his latest solved homicide. Zimmer looks over at Liam and yells,

"You see, I did get my own lucky charm!"

Liam thinks to himself, we've come a long way for the first day.

———⊸∘⊷———

Liam continues to drive northbound on Interstate 95, smiling as he remembers the first time he met Zim. I learned a lot from that old man, he thought. He continues to think back to the retirement party he

99

threw Zim a year later, and how Kelley cooked dinner for him at their home every third Thursday of the month until his death two years later. At Zim's funeral, Liam learned that it was Gordon Zimmer who asked Lieutenant Mahoney to partner them up. The lieutenant never told either one of us the truth. Just why did he partner us up? On the face of it, we were the odd couple, yet the chemistry somehow worked.

He glances down at the report while taking a bite of jerky, and continues to drive in the rain. He thinks back to the start of the investigation into the murder of Lonnie Theodore Jackson...

"O'Connor, Zim, get your sorry asses in my office," yells Lt. Mahoney from his office.

"What the fuck did you do now, Liam? It's four-thirty on Friday. We're not on call this week, we pulled the last homicide, so we should be good to go for the weekend.

I know you fucked something up, Liam," says Zim while looking at Liam.

They continue to walk towards the lieutenant's office.

"We've had more cases in the last six months than I had in the year and half prior to you being my partner," says Zim.

"That's because you were on the junior varsity team before. Now you're playing with the big boys, so shut the fuck up!" says Liam as they sit down in the lieutenant's office.

"Liam," says the lieutenant.

"See, see what I mean?" asks Zim while shaking his head.

The lieutenant continues, "Liam, do you know a detention officer by the name of Ed Ramirez?"

"Yes, I coached him at Brighton High many years ago. I didn't know he worked for the department, though," says Liam.

"He has some information about a possible murder from one of his inmate laborers at the detention facility in South Boston. Apparently, Ramirez was told by a female I.L. about a murder that took place at an automobile dismantling business in the Jamaica Plains suburb," says Lt. Mahoney.

"I want the two of you to talk with Ramirez and see if there is anything to this, or not."

"Lieutenant," says Zim, "the last time you sent us out to the jail to talk to someone about a murder, he told us that he and Charlie Manson killed and ate two Puerto Rican kids at Fenway Park. He went on to tell us that he distrusted all people and that he was currently having nightly sex with his German shepherd. Sir, these fuckers will say anything to get out of jail."

"You're right, Zim, they will. And sometimes they rat on others to save their own ass," says Lieutenant Mahoney.

"Okay, sir, we'll go check it out and let you know what's going on," says Liam.

The two detectives leave the lieutenant's office and drive to the detention facility.

Once at the facility, they are led into the office of the facility commander, who meets them and explains that Detention Officer Ramirez is in route to his office from the kitchen area. A short time later, Ramirez arrives and meets the two detectives.

"Coach O, I haven't seen you in a long time," says Ramirez. "I read that Brighton High won the city championship again," he laughs.

"We did all right this year, Pork Chop!" says Liam.

Zim, the commander, and Liam all laugh.

"You remembered," says Ramirez.

"I picked this guy up every Saturday morning during football season and drove him to school for film study. Every time I came to pick him up, he was eating a pork chop, so it kind of stuck with him," says Liam as he reaches over and hugs Ramirez. "So, I hear you have some info for us."

"Maybe, Coach, I don't know. It sounds good to me, but I thought I would at least forward it on and let someone with a higher pay grade make the decision," says Ramirez.

"You did the right thing, Ed," says the commander.

"Sir, I'm assigned as the coordinator for the inmate laborers in the facility. Basically, I select who has earned the privilege to be an I.L. within the facility, and then I place them in work assignments as needed. I.L.s earn credits off their time served, and they get other compensation that other inmates don't," says Ramirez.

"Like what special compensation?" asks Zim.

Ramirez responds, "Well, sir, if they're on the car wash crew, they get to be outside instead of being locked up, so it depends on what the assignment is as to the perks of the job. Earlier today, one of my female I.L.s assigned to the kitchen asked to speak with me. This happens all the time, because inmates want to be transferred to another position or just removed as an inmate laborer. So I met with inmate Rosemary Cantu. She told me her cellmate and girlfriend, Maria Rodriquez, told her she was in danger while in this facility. Cantu said before Rodriquez was busted for drugs and prostitution, she was with two white guys in the Jamaica Plains. Rodriquez told her they all partied at this compound for several days. Cantu told me that Rodriquez sells herself for money and/or drugs when she's on the outside, but this time when the drugs were gone after two days, those guys felt she used more drugs than she was worth. She went on to tell me that they kept Rodriquez against her will. Rodriquez was told the only way she would be allowed to leave was to call someone who would bring a hundred bucks she owed for the drugs she used."

Zim says, "So far this sounds like a civil problem. I mean, this chick is playing everybody and sniffing both sides of the bench, if you know what I mean."

"Go on, Ed," laughs Liam, "don't mind him."

Ramirez continues, "Cantu said Rodriquez called a guy she knew from Charlestown to come and pick her up. Apparently when this guy arrived, they robbed and killed him. Cantu went on to say that Rodriquez is in fear for her life in this facility and didn't want to tell anyone."

"It sounds like we need to at least talk with this lady," says Liam.

"Lady," says Zim. "I bet she's fucking a German shepherd too!"

"Don't mind him," says Liam.

"I'll have Rodriquez brought to the interview room for you two," says the commander.

Liam continues driving on I-95 and thinks, I need fuel and a bite to eat. Jacksonville is up the road twenty miles, and this looks like a good place to stop and shake the dew off the lily. Liam continues on to Jacksonville and stops. He fills the Cruiser and eats some jerky. He remembers how Kelley couldn't believe that he would eat jerky and drink Gatorade for a meal. Working crime scenes for many years had taught Liam what to pack in his war bag to get him through long periods where there was little food or drink available. A quick restroom break and the taking of his daily medication, and Liam is back on the road. Northbound Interstate 95—next stop, Florence, South Carolina.

Having gathered some personal belongings from her residence, Tina returns to the condo and has successfully checked every cabinet and drawer in Liam's place to learn more about him. She finds Liam's family photos, along with articles about various murder investigations conducted by Liam and his partners. Looking at the photos, she sees a tired-looking man toward the end of his career. Tina also discovers another bit of information she was wanting to know: his underwear of choice, boxers. That's what I thought, she thinks.

She lies down on the couch and watches "Woman of the Year," an older movie featuring Spencer Tracy and Katherine Hepburn. She falls asleep a short time into the movie while Sandy sits and watches from her favorite chair, expecting Liam to return home at any minute.

CHAPTER 6

SEVEN CIGS FOR SISTER MARIA

LIAM DRIVES ON TOWARD FLORENCE, South Carolina, as he looks down at the murder book and remembers back.

————◦◦◦————

Zim and Liam walk to the interview room and sit down behind a long table. Liam tells Zim,

"Let me do most of the talking. You just sit there for now." They wait for a few minutes when they both see through the glass door window that a woman is being escorted down the hallway toward them.

"Are you fucking kidding me?" says Zim. "I see why they wanted more money."

"That's one door-full of a woman," says Liam. "Who knows, Zim, maybe she has skills. How much money you got on you?" laughs Liam.

The door opens and the detention officer says, "Okay! Detectives, this is Maria Rodriquez," as he sits her down at the table.

"Detectives," she says, "who are you guys?"

Liam pushes a business card across the corner of the table. Rodriquez looks at the card that reads Liam O'Connor, Detective, Homicide Unit, Boston Police Department.

Liam says, "This is my partner, Detective Gordon Zimmer."

Liam stops talking. They sit for a few seconds without saying a word. Rodriquez starts to fidget in her seat. She looks at Liam and Zim several times, and then down at the floor while taking a deep breath.

Liam says, "I'm going to read you something, and as I do, you need to think real hard on whether you want to help yourself out or not. You have the right to remain silent. Anything you say can and will be used against you in a court of law. You have the right to an attorney and to have that attorney present before and during questioning, if you desire. If you cannot afford an attorney, one will be appointed to represent you. Do you understand these rights I've explained to you?" asks Liam.

Rodriquez answers, "Yes I do."

Liam and Zim say nothing, but they continue to stare at Rodriquez for a few seconds. Rodriquez says, "I'll talk to you, but when we're done, you gotta see if you can transfer me outta here or I'm dead. I want one other thing."

"What?" asks Liam.

"I want a pack of cigarettes to take back to my cell, for me and my baby girl."

"Tobacco products are a violation of the facility rules," says Liam.

"They'll never know I have them," says Rodriquez.

"We'll see," says Liam.

Again, there's an awkward few seconds of silence.

"About six days ago, I was called by a girlfriend who told me there were some brothers staying in a small garage in the center of an auto dismantling yard in the Jamaica Plains area. She told me these guys had recently got out of prison and were holding lots of meth. She said they drove a tow truck and lived inside this compound in Jamaica Plains. I live in JP, so I got a ride over to this place," says Rodriquez.

"What was the name of the dismantling yard?" asks Liam.

"Liberty Dismantling, off Rock Hill Road," says Rodriquez.

"I got there at about nine o'clock on Friday night. The place has a tall fence around the property and an office near the front entrance. I was told to walk back through the yard toward the center of the yard, where there would be a small house or shack with a shit-load of auto parts, tools, engine hoists, and car tires all around. When I got to the shack, I thought my friend Yvonne would be there, but she wasn't. Then this big peckerwood came from the house and asked if I was Maria. He brought me into the house, where I met his brother. Both guys were tatted up with all kinds of prison tattoos."

Rodriquez said she'd seen the same tats before and thought they were from a white supremacist group known as the 'White Wolves of West Virginia.'

The two brothers were bald, and both had tats on their necks that read WWWV with a circled cross. They both had a large wolf tattooed in the center of their backs.

Liam asks, "Did they tell you they were brothers, or because they looked similar, you thought they were?"

Rodriquez replies, "The first guy that brought me into the house, his name was Bobby Dale, and pointed to a second guy who was shooting up meth and said, 'That's my brother, Randall Dale.'"

"Was that their full name, or do you have a last name too?" asks Zimmer.

"I'm not sure I got the last name right. They never told me their last names, but I think it was tattooed on their forearms. All the tattoos had others over the top of them, so it was hard to make out the name, but I think it read Pentacast, Pentecoss, Pente-something, I'm just not sure what. I asked where Yvonne was and one of them said, 'We kicked that stinky bitch out,'" says Rodriquez.

"What happened then?" asks Liam.

Rodriquez says she fucked them both for about an hour or so while stopping to do more meth from time to time.

"I snort meth, but these guys were shooting it up," she says. "We partied through the night until the next morning, when we all crashed for a few hours till the afternoon."

Rodriquez says she told the brothers that she had to leave, so she could go to work. She says that Bobby Dale told her she couldn't leave. "He said that I was 'a fat Puerto Rican cow that wasn't worth the fucking drugs I snorted.'" She says Bobby Dale told her she owed them at least a hundred for the drugs she used. She didn't have the money on her, but could get it and bring it back. Randall Dale told her to call someone that would bring money to her, because she wasn't leaving until they got what was owed them.

"Who did you call?" asks Zim.

"I have a sugar daddy that I see every week. He lives in a condo in Charlestown, and he has lots of money. He used to work for the post office for like forty years or something. I thought he would come, pick me up, and pay these two peckerwoods their money. I called Lonnie, Lonnie Jackson, and asked if he would pick me up from the dismantling yard."

"How long have you known Jackson?" asks Liam.

"I've been fucking him on and off for about six years. You see, he's an older guy in his sixties, and he don't mind if I sleep with men or women. He just wants to be taken care of," says Rodriquez.

"I can understand that. Can you relate to that, Zim?" laughs Liam.

Rodriquez said, "I called Jackson and told him where I was, and he agreed to pick me up."

"Did you tell him about the money that he needed to have?" asks Liam.

"No," says Rodriquez, "I was afraid he wouldn't show."

"Forty-minutes later, Lonnie's Cadillac pulled down the dirt road toward the shack. She and the brothers walked out of the house toward the moving car. As the car got closer, Bobby Dale yelled, 'You called a fucking nigger here?' She says when Bobby Dale saw that Lonnie was black, he lost it. When Lonnie stopped his car in front of the shack, Bobby Dale walked toward the driver's side of the car and said, 'You're one dead fucking nigger.'"

Rodriquez said, "Bobby Dale had a knife in his right hand and reached into the car and stabbed Lonnie once in the left side of his neck. He continued to stab him at least three more times in the chest. Bobby Dale said to Randall, 'I broke the blade off in his chest.'

Rodriquez continued, "She says, 'I saw Lonnie slump over toward the passenger side of the car while the car was still running. I thought the brothers were going to kill me then, for bringing Lonnie there.'"

"Did they ever say anything to you about the color of your skin...I mean, you being Puerto Rican and all?" asks Zimmer.

"No. I guess because I'm light complexioned, they never said anything," says Rodriquez. "Once Lonnie wasn't moving or making any noise, Randall Dale said to Bobby, we need to get him and his car the fuck out of here. Bobby Dale told me to remove Lonnie's wallet and see how much money he had. So I removed his wallet from Lonnie's front pocket and pulled the cash out. I gave all the cash to Bobby Dale. Randall Dale said he had a place to dump the body in South Boston. He said he would drive Lonnie's Cadillac, with Lonnie and I in the back seat, while Bobby Dale would follow in the tow truck. The brothers put Lonnie in the back seat behind the driver's side and then told me to sit in the front with Randall. Randall told his brother to grab some tow chains and other car parts and put them in the trunk before they left the yard."

"How much money did you pull off of Lonnie?" asks Zim.

Rodriquez says, "He had about eighty-five dollars on him. We left the yard on Rock Hill and drove across town to the shipyards in South Boston. Randall and Bobby Dale pulled Lonnie's body from the back seat. They put chains around his neck and hooked heavy metal parts to a chain and wrapped it around his waist and legs. They fucking rolled Lonnie's body over the side of the dock and into the water."

"Did you see anyone around the yards when you pulled up to the docks?" asks Liam.

Rodriquez replies, "No, I didn't see anyone around, but we weren't there for very long. After they dumped his body, I thought they were going to kill me, but Randall told me to get back into the Cadillac, so I did. Randall followed Bobby Dale out of the shipyards and we drove to the Chinatown area, where he let me out. I called a friend from Chinatown who came and gave me a ride back to my house."

"Have you had any contact with either Bobby Dale or Randall Dale since they dropped you off in Chinatown?" asks Liam.

"No, I don't want to see those fuckers ever again," says Rodriquez.

"Why are you so afraid of staying in this facility? I mean, you told us you wanted to be transferred, but why?" asks Zimmer.

"When we were partying, Randall Dale said his mother worked at the jail in South Boston," says Rodriquez.

"Doing what?" asks Zim.

"I don't know. I don't even know if it's true or not," says Rodriquez.

"How did you end up in here? I mean, why were you arrested?" asks Liam.

"On Tuesday, I got stopped walking in the Plains and was holding some methamphetamine. They slapped a solicitation charge on me too, so I ended up here waiting to go to court."

"Would you be able to show us the place where Lonnie was dumped at, and the dismantling yard in Jamaica Plains?" asks Liam.

"Yeah, I guess so," says Rodriquez.

"Now, Maria, think about this question real carefully before you answer it. Did you keep any of the money or credit cards from Lonnie's wallet? Remember, it's very possible that we've already talked to either Bobby Dale or Randall Dale, and they may have told us a different story about the money," says Liam. "Think about this, Maria, why are we here?" asks Liam. Zim and Liam look at Rodriquez and smile.

"They gave me thirty dollars and one of his credit cards, and told me if I said anything they would kill me. I spent the money, but I had the card on me when I was arrested," says Rodriquez.

"Okay, what we're going to do is check some of your story out and arrange to get you out of here, so you can show us where Lonnie was dumped," says Liam. "Until then, we'll have you placed in protective custody and put into a single cell."

"Hey, you guys owe me something!" says Rodriquez.

"All I have is seven cigs left in this pack," says Zim. "I promise if what you've told us leads us to Lonnie Jackson, I'll buy you a carton of cigarettes."

"Okay. I'll take those seven cigs now, though," says Rodriquez.

"How will you get them back to the cell without getting busted on a search?" asks Zim. He removes all of his cigarettes from his last pack and gives them to Rodriquez. Rodriquez reaches down and puts her right hand underneath her jail pants, and smiles as she secures the cigarettes in her vagina. Liam and Zim get up from the table, open the interview door and summon a detention officer.

"Please place her back into protective custody, single cell if you can," requests Liam.

Rodriquez is escorted down the hall away from Liam and Zim.

Zim turns to Liam and says, "Witness, my ass! She called Lonnie there to rob him and got caught up in a murder."

Liam replies, "Hey, it'll be up to the D.A. on whether she's a witness or an accomplice, but she's fucking dirty if you ask me. She sold out Bobby and Randall Dale for seven cigarettes, Zim. I'll brief the facility commander on what we found out and see if he can arrange to have a female detentions officer accompany us to the shipyards to locate Jackson. In the meantime, see if there's been a missing person's report made out on Jackson," says Liam.

"I'm on it like a hobo on a ham sandwich, Liam," says Zim.

"I guess this means no Friday night boom-boom for you," says Liam.

"Fucked again," says Zimmer.

The two split up and soon find each other back in the facility commander's office.

"A missing person's report was filed three days ago on a Lonnie Theodore Jackson. A black male, sixty-seven years old, living in Charlestown off School Street," says Zim.

"Listed on the missing person's report was Jackson's red 1984 Cadillac Deville, Massachusetts license 3R-3821."

"Good job, Zim. I've arranged for a female detentions officer as an escort for Rodriquez, and for the dive team to meet us at the shipyards in South Boston," says Liam.

"Liam, I'll bet she asks for something more before she shows us where Jackson was dumped," says Zim.

"Could be, Zim...but we need that body, or we don't have shit. We have nothing more than a story, unless we locate Randall or Bobby Dale and they cooperate," says Liam.

Rodriquez and a female detentions officer meet up with Liam and Zim in the parking lot of the South Boston Detention Facility. They leave the facility and drive in the unmarked detective's vehicle toward the shipyards.

Rodriquez states, "You guys are going to transfer me out of South Boston, right? I mean, I can't stay there after this."

"How do you know what Bobby and Randall Dale told you, about their mother working at the jail, was even the truth?" asks Zimmer.

"I don't, but why would they lie to me?"

Liam looks at Zim and says, "She's right, there's no reason to drop that information on her. They gain nothing by telling her that."

Rodriquez directs them to an area off 16th Street, near the docks to one of many shipyards in the Charlestown, South Boston, area. They stop their vehicle and get out. Rodriquez walks over to the edge of the dock and says,

"This is it. This is where they rolled him over."

Zim and Liam look at each other in surprise and disbelief.

"What do you think?" asks Zim.

"She didn't even have to look around. I mean, bam! The first stop, this is it. She's fucking playing us," says Zim, out of earshot of Rodriquez.

Liam looks over the dock's edge and sees murky water. He calls for the police dive

123

team to respond to his location. Liam is told it will be about twenty minutes before they'll arrive.

"I'm so glad I called them ahead of time, or we'd be waiting an hour or more," says Liam.

"Zim, take the unit and get some burgers and drinks for us all. I'll stay here with the ladies. It's getting late, and we could be here a while."

Liam takes Zimmer to the side, away from the women, gives Zim two twenties and says, "I want change back this time...no booze for you! Just straight Coke."

Zim takes the money, smiles and drives off.

Twenty minutes pass and the dive team arrives and starts to set up lights and check equipment. Liam briefs the lieutenant in charge of the team and explains the possible location of a homicide victim. A short time later, Zim returns with several bags of food and drinks from McDonald's. The lieutenant tells Liam they'll drop a long pole with a camera attached down the side of the dock and see if they can locate the body before divers hit the water. Zim begins to dole out the food and drinks to Rodriquez, the detention officer, himself, and Liam. He takes Liam aside, returns the change and tells Liam, "A bottle of Jack they can't find the body."

"You're on. But if they do, I'll take Jameson," says Liam.

Liam walks over to the dive team and stands near the camera monitor. The camera is dropped into the water near the point Rodriquez indicated Jackson's body was dumped. After a brief search of three to five minutes, the body is located. There are several chains and car alternators wrapped around the head and upper torso. The body is on the floor of the ocean, which is about thirty-five feet deep. Liam turns to Zimmer and says, "Zim, they found him. Come here and see!"

"I told you he was there," says Rodriquez, as she continues eating her hamburger like it was her last meal. Liam looks at Rodriquez, who continues to eat, grabbing more fries.

Liam says, "You don't need to be transferred to another jail, you need to be taken to a zoo!" shaking his head in disgust.

The dive team deploys and retrieves the body of Lonnie Theodore Jackson. The coroner examines the body for injuries prior to being transported to the morgue. Jackson has sustained a single stab wound to the left side of his neck and several stab wounds to his chest, like Maria Rodriquez said. Jackson was transported to the morgue for further examination. Now with the body of Jackson located, Zimmer and Liam's next task was to identify and to locate Bobby Dale and Randall Dale.

"Let's head back to the jail and make arrangements for Rodriquez to be transferred," says Liam. They transport Rodriquez back to the South Boston Detention Facility. While Rodriquez is being escorted back to her cell, the facility commander speaks with Zim and Liam. He tells Liam that he printed out a list of all his employees, both sworn personnel and civilian staff, per Liam's request.

"What the fuck is this?" asks Zim.

Liam says, "Zim, she was afraid that the brother's mother worked here. Check the list and see if we still have the luck of the Irish with us tonight. Look for a woman with the last name of Pentacast, Pente-something."

Zimmer looks through the list of employees while Liam calls Lieutenant Johnson and briefs him on the status of the investigation. While Liam is talking to the lieutenant, Zimmer says, "Un-fucking believable," and points to a name on the list.

Liam hangs the phone up and turns to Zimmer.

"What?" he asks.

Zim shows him the list of names and points to Connie Pentecost, a kitchen specialist, currently working the morning shift. Liam asks the facility commander if he has access to the computer personnel files. He says, "Yes what would you like to know about Connie Pentecost?"

"How old is she?" asks Liam.

The commander accesses a computer and starts to search the employees' data file.

"Okay, I got her here in the system. Let's see, she's...forty-nine," says the commander.

"That would be about right," says Zim. "Does she list any relatives on any of her emergency contact forms?"

"Yes, she lists three children. A daughter, Cathy, and two sons, Bobby Dale and Randall Dale Pentecost," says the commander.

"Bingo, we have a bingo! Luck of the Irish, Zim," says Liam.

Zim says, "I'll bet the brothers have a record someplace. Commander, do you have the ability to check individual's arrest records on your computer here?" asks Zim.

"I sure do," says the commander. "Let me check and see the last time they've been arrested."

"We are assuming they have been arrested," says Liam.

"These fuckers have been arrested. The information Rodriquez gave us was spot on," says Zim. "She said she saw both of the brothers with what she thought were prison tattoos on their back and arms, remember?"

"They're in our system," says the commander. "They were both arrested three days ago in Charlestown."

"For what?" asks Liam.

"Possession of stolen property, and possession of a controlled substance, Methamphetamine," says the facility commander.

"Oh shit! What?"asks Zim and Liam,

"They're currently being housed here." The facility commander looks at Liam and Zim, and says, "They're here, just two floors up."

"Let's get some photos of the brothers and confirm with Rodriquez that they are our guys before she gets transported outta here in the next hour or so," says Liam.

———◁◦▷———

I'm on track and making good time, thinks Liam. I'm in Florence, South Carolina, at three-thirty in the morning. I need a Starbucks, though. That shit will keep me amped up for a few hours. He fills the Cruiser with fuel, sees a

Starbucks across the freeway and heads that way. He laughs as he thinks back to the Jackson case and the sheer dumb luck that came their way during the investigation. He remembers how Zim swaggered around the detective division for a week, declaring how he and Liam had solved an unreported murder for seven cigarettes. Liam thinks back to how Zim was proud that he was relevant again, not just an old, burned-out drunk.

Liam gets his favorite coffee, a plain black Grande, and remembers how Kelley would tease him for just getting a plain coffee. Never willing to try the other blended drinks that they were so well known for. He thinks back to what he would always tell her: "I know what I like, that's why I stay with it. I've been married to you for over thirty years, haven't I?" Kelley would just smile and hug him. Wrapping her arms around his waist, she would tell him, "You've kissed the Blarney Stone a few too many times, my husband, but you can warm my bed anytime."

Liam starts back on the road, thinking that his next stop should be Richmond, Virginia. He wants to call T.J. and ask if the dead visitor in Port Saint Lucie is either the son or relative of Bobby Dale

Pentecost or Randall Dale Pentecost, currently residing in Hazelton United States Penitentiary in West Virginia. Liam decides to wait a few more hours until it's eight or nine a.m. in Boston.

Liam remembers that once Maria Rodriquez identified the brothers, they refused to talk with him and Zim. Six months after the brothers were charged with first-degree murder, Liam testified in Boston's Federal Court, for five days, on the murder of Lonnie Theodore Jackson. The Federal prosecutor decided that the two white supremacist brothers should be tried in Federal court under a new hate crime act brought into law early in the '90's. The Boston Police Department and the Attorney General's Office got lots of good PR out of the capture and conviction of the Pentecost brothers. The brothers were found guilty of first-degree murder and sentenced to life without parole. After the brothers were found guilty, the prosecutor allowed Maria Rodriquez to plea to second-degree murder. Maria was sentenced to ten years in a Federal prison, with a chance at early parole. Liam and Zim each gave Rodriquez a carton of cigarettes as she was loaded onto the bus and headed for Federal prison.

CHAPTER 7

HANGING BY A THREAD

LIAM CONTINUES HIS DRIVE TO BOSTON, planning his next stop to be in Newark, New Jersey. I'll call T.J. then, maybe he can get me some answers as to why this kid is after me now. He thinks about Sandy and how she's doing with Tina. Tina has brought back feelings he had only shared with Kelley. He's not sure just how to react to her. He feels as though he's being unfaithful to Kelley for letting himself feel again for another woman. I'm a mess, he thinks. My hands shake like I'm jacking off a squirrel, I'll cry if I smell something that reminds me of Kelley, and yet I can't deny the attraction to Tina. He also knows if he doesn't figure out who wants him dead, none of this will be a problem much longer.

The long drive continues from state to state until reaching the next scheduled stop in Newark. Liam refills the Cruiser and buys more jerky and Gatorade. He calls T.J. from the pay phone in the parking lot of a Dunkin' Donuts shop.

"T.J., my brother."

"Liam, are you all right?" asks T.J.

"Yeah, I'm hanging in there. T.J., I'm headed back to Boston. I'm in Newark now, so I've gotten or so more hours before I get there. Can you check something out for me, please?" asks Liam.

"Anything for you...what do you need?" replies T.J.

"First, tell no one you've heard from me...no one at all, no matter who asks. Understand T.J.?" says Liam.

"I got it, Liam. You don't trust anyone, do you?" asks T.J.

"I trust you with my life," says Liam.

"Second, can you see if the dead subject you identified to me last night as Bobby Dale Pentecost has any listed family on his prison records? I'm wanting to know his relationship to the Bobby Dale Pentecost I put in the penitentiary over twenty years ago," says Liam.

"Do you think it's his son?" asks T.J.

"It makes sense," says Liam. "I'll call you back in about three to four hours and see what you've found out."

"Liam, I look forward to seeing you again. I've missed you these past months," says T.J.

"I've missed you too. Hey, when the time is right, we'll hoist a few to those who are no longer with us," says Liam.

"You remember what Dad used to say?"

"When we drink, we get drunk. When we get drunk, we fall asleep. When we fall asleep, we commit no sin. When we commit no sin, we go to heaven. So, let's all get drunk and go to heaven!" "That might be the only way I can sleep these days, T.J.," says Liam.

"Still can't sleep, Liam?" asks T.J.

"You know you need to see a doctor."

"I'm afraid to sleep, T.J. I'm afraid to dream. I see Kelley in my dreams. The hardest part is waking up and realizing she's gone...she's gone. I just miss her," says Liam.

"I wonder if I told her I loved her enough? If I was a good husband to her, was she happy? I should have danced more with her. Every damn day I think of this!"

"One day at a time, Liam," says T.J.

"Some days are better than others. I'll call you in a little while, talk to you then. Goodbye," says Liam.

Liam drives on to his next planned stop in Hartford, Connecticut.

Two hours of driving and Liam remembers he must take his daily medication. He stops at a roadside store and takes his pills. He looks over and sees a pay phone, and decides to call Tina. I'll call her to check on Sandy, thinks Liam. He starts to dial Tina's phone number and oddly, he starts to get nervous about what to say.

"Hello, Tina, this is Liam. I'm doing fine, thanks for asking. No, I'm not tired yet. I just called to see how you and Sandy are getting along. Yeah, I should have told you she likes to sleep on the bed. Yes, I'm taking my medications. How'd you know about that? Oh, I see. I'm sorry there's not much food in the fridge. She did... no! Tina, it's okay, it's fine. I'll call her back soon. Thanks for everything.

136

I'll call back soon to check on you two. That's my plan, Tina. I plan on being back as soon as I can."

Liam hangs the phone up and thinks to himself, there's something about that woman. He continues driving on, knowing that Molley called and spoke with Tina this morning. Molley wanted to know where he was and if he had started back to Boston already. Uncle Henry, the informer! Well, if Molley knows, Mama does too, thinks Liam. No time to deal with it.

<hr />

"Hello, yes ma'am, this is Officer Youngblood, but please call me Tina. She did... yes, that's right, I'm watching Sandy for a few days. Well, I have a couple of days off, so I thought I would help Mr. O'Connor. Yes, ma'am, Liam left last night. Uh, I could come out and see you at around noon, if that's a good time for you, Mrs. O'Connor. Okay, I'll see you then, ma'am." Tina hangs up the phone. What have I gotten myself into, she thinks. Well, Tina, just be yourself. God has a plan, so deal with it.

Tina looks at Sandy and says,

"I better get you fed and walked before I head out and see Mrs. O'Connor."

Tina places a leash on Sandy and starts out the front door. They begin to walk around the complex and are met by residents who ask about Sandy and Liam. Tina learns that Liam is known in their small community as the dog walker. Apparently, he walks other residents' dogs when their owners are unable to. Tina gets a sense that Liam is well-liked in the community. The shooting at his place has caused the rumors to run wild. She wonders what they will say now.

⟨⟩

Hartford, Connecticut, at last, thinks Liam. I'll stop and get some solid food, and call T.J. Liam pulls off the freeway and gets some gas for the Toyota. Wintertime in the north, thinks Liam. He's always liked the colder weather in Boston and the northeast, but he can't help thinking about how Kelley died. Liam crosses the street and pulls into the parking lot of a restaurant called The Idle Spur Bar and Grill. I could go for a shot of Jameson and a pint of Guinness, he thinks. He knows he has a few hours' drive before he reaches Boston, so food only. He calls T.J. from a pay phone near the bar.

"Hello, T.J... yeah, I'm in Hartford, so I'm a couple hours away. Did you find anything out? That's what we thought... Bobby Dale Pentecost is the son. He was a junior, then. What do you mean, not really? His father and his uncle, Randall Dale, were killed in a gang riot six months ago at the United States Penitentiary in Hazelton, West Virginia? That explains some things, T.J. You got a letter for me? Who sent it? When was it sent to you? You got it today, but it was mailed out two days ago from Nickolas Torigiani? I thought Captain Torigiani was still in custody? Okay. T.J., I'll be in Boston in a few hours. Yeah, that's my first stop, I'll call you from there,"

Liam enters the restaurant and orders a meal. He remembers Captain Torigiani was a close friend of his father's and wonders if the captain is aware of his father's death. Nick Torigiani was found guilty of second-degree murder about seven years ago. Torigiani stabbed to death Boston's assistant district attorney, at that time, Alton Mills. Mills' death occurred during the time Liam was recovering from a gunshot wound. Liam remembers being thankful he didn't have to arrest Captain Torigiani. His father and Torigiani had been close in their earlier years on the force, but drifted apart as Captain T. was promoted through the ranks. He finishes his meal and starts back on the road, knowing his final stop is a few hours away. He continues to drive to Boston, wondering why Pentecost and Shea would have envelopes containing hundred-dollar bills—unless someone was paying them.

CHAPTER 8

COFFEE, COOKIES, AND CHEMISTRY

TINA ARRIVES AT THE CARRIAGE HOUSE assisted living facility. She enters the front doors and walks to Mrs. O'Connor's room, but stops before knocking. Just be yourself, Tina, she thinks. She knocks on the door, and a short time later the door opens. Mrs. O'Connor, speaking in her soft Irish Boston accent, says,

"Please come in, Officer Youngblood."

"Call me Tina, ma'am. I'm not working now."

Tina slowly walks through the door.

"Tina, please sit with me in the living room. I'm so worried about Liam. I thought you might be able to clear some things up."

"I would be glad to, if I can, ma'am."

141

"Oh, call me Maggie."

"Okay, Maggie it is."

"Did Liam tell you anything about who he was going to see in Boston?" asks Mrs. O'Connor.

"No, he didn't. He said he would be gone for awhile, and asked if I would watch Sandy," says Tina. "He asked if I'd like to stay at his place while watching her. He thought it might be easier to just stay there. He really said very little before he left."

"That's my Liam," says Mrs. O'Connor. "The quiet one. Liam wasn't much for words before Kelley's death, but after her death he's not let many people through that wall he put up. My fear is that he'll slip deeper and deeper into his own abyss, until one day, we'll lose him," says Mrs. O'Connor. "You're my ray of hope, Tina. For Liam to ask you to stay at his place and watch that old dog means, to me, he has some feelings for you. He's interested in you. Molley called and told me about talking to you," says Mrs. O'Connor.

"Ma'am, I don't mean to cause any problems for Liam and his daughter. I'll leave Liam's place," says Tina.

"Tina, you'll do no such thing. Molley and I are happy about this new *situation*. I'll just leave it as a situation right now," says Mrs. O'Connor with a smile.

"Would you like some tea or coffee, and cookies? I'm going to have some. Please have some."

"Yes, coffee please," replies Tina.

Mrs. O'Connor walks slowly over from the dining room area to the kitchen, pours coffee into two cups, and prepares a plate of homemade cookies. Tina looks toward the kitchen and asks if she needs help with anything. Mrs. O'Connor sticks her head back into the living room with a bottle of Jameson whiskey in her hand and asks Tina if she'd like an Irish coffee. Tina tells Mrs. O'Connor just a plain black coffee would be fine. Tina looks toward the kitchen and sees Mrs. O'Connor pour a little whiskey and brown sugar into her own cup of coffee, and then stir the cup with a spoon. She watches as Mrs. O'Connor returns from the kitchen. Mrs. O'Connor hands Tina her cup of black coffee while she begins to sip her special coffee.

"I have a little snoot every day. It thins the blood and keeps me young," says Mrs.

O'Connor. "Joseph, Liam's father, drank Jameson and Irish beer like most people drink milk. Like a lot of Irish men, Joseph grew up with a pub mentality. When Liam was growing up, I used to tell Liam to go and get his father from his favorite pub two or three times a week. It's the culture with Irish men. Instead of going home after work, they would go to the local pub, have a few, and then maybe come home."

"Ma'am, I mean Maggie, when I was here earlier with Lieutenant Tibedoe, I saw a photo on the wall with two men in uniform," says Tina.

"Oh! Yes, that's Liam and his father," says Maggie.

She and Tina walk over to a wall near the kitchen, and Mrs. O'Connor removes several pictures from the wall as they walk back to the living room and sit. Mrs. O'Connor sips her coffee and tells Tina that the photo of Joseph and Liam was taken when Liam graduated from the police academy.

"That photo was one of Joseph's favorites. Mine is his graduation photo from Boston University," says Maggie.

Mrs. O'Connor tells Tina that Joseph wanted their eldest son, James, to be a police officer. She tells Tina that Jimmy was killed in Vietnam. She goes on to say that the death of Jimmy took a toll on them all.

"Joseph drank more, Liam talked less, and I went to church. That war took a little from all of us. It seems the O'Connors hide their emotions, each in their own way," says Maggie.

"Tina, did you know that Liam and his father worked together for a short time, when Liam was a rookie patrol officer? Liam had big shoes to fill within the department. His father worked the streets through rough times for twenty-plus years before Liam came along. Liam's first shooting was with his father in Dorchester," says Mrs. O'Connor. "Dorchester, Boston, in the '80s was a very diverse community, still mostly African Americans. Liam was known in the community as a football player and coach, but now he was dealing with people as a cop. I think he earned respect from the different communities of Boston as a police officer through his fairness to all, something his father taught him," says Mrs. O'Connor.

"Tina, would you like more coffee or anything?"

"No, I'm fine, Maggie," says Tina. "What happened with Liam and his father in Dorchester?"

"Oh," Mrs. O'Connor says, "I'm sorry. Where was I? Oh, yes. One summer night, they were dispatched to a woman screaming at an apartment complex. When they arrived, they were met by several residents who told them a woman on the third floor was screaming that her husband was stabbing her. A neighbor told Liam and Joseph that the man and his wife fight all the time. She told them her husband used dope, and when he does, he gets crazy. Liam and Joseph go to the third floor and see people standing in their doorways, pointing to the door of an apartment. Liam knocks and announces who they are, but is told to go away. They stood outside the front door. Both could smell something god-awful burning inside the apartment. Joseph kicked in the front door, and Liam and Joseph entered the apartment. They walked toward the kitchen area and saw the wife lying on the floor near the kitchen table. She'd been stabbed multiple times in the chest and face, including having her throat cut open

146

from ear to ear. The woman's left breast had been cut off. Joseph told me that the blood flowed from one side of the kitchen floor to the other. He said he hadn't seen a sight like that since Korea. Liam continued into the kitchen and saw the husband, nude, standing over the stove." Mrs. O'Connor stops for a moment, shakes her head, and then continues on with the story. "Liam and Joseph see the husband is armed with a foot-long, one-inch-wide boning knife. The husband is standing over the stove, frying something in a large pan. Liam orders the man to drop the knife, but he refused to. Joseph told me the smell in the kitchen coming from the frying pan was unbearable. He said it sounded like someone was frying bacon, because of the hissing and popping sound coming from the pan. Liam looked into the pan and saw the husband was frying his two-month-old baby. Liam shot the man twice in the chest and twice in the head. Joseph said as the man slumped to the ground, Liam fired twice more into his head. Liam removed the baby from the pan, but the baby was burnt too badly to survive. They tried to save the mother, but she bled out in their arms on the kitchen floor. After the investigation was completed, it was found that the husband was under the influence of something called PCP," says Mrs. O'Connor.

Mrs. O'Connor went on to tell Tina that an investigation into the shooting took place, as per Boston Police policy, on all officer-involved shootings. She said the community in Dorchester was angry at the officers and the department for the shooting.

"Tina, would you like more coffee, or perhaps more cookies?" asks Mrs. O'Connor.

"No, Maggie, I'm doing fine," says Tina. "Didn't the department explain to the public what happened?" she asks, looking at Mrs. O'Connor with great interest.

"Well, they finally did just that. Liam and Joseph were suspended until the investigation into the shooting was completed. With the community in Dorchester demanding answers, Police Commissioner Fitzpatrick called a press conference and told the people of Boston how and why the shooting occurred. Tina, the Commissioner should have won an Academy Award. If you weren't in tears at the end of that press conference, you'd better have yourself checked. The community of Dorchester came out in solid support of the department. Joseph and Liam were never to work together again. The department publicly gave them awards for valor, but what most people didn't know was that Liam received several days' suspension."

"For what?" asks Tina.

"Liam was found to have been outside of department policy, having shot two additional times into the head of the husband. Joseph always said that Liam had been baptized into department politics. Liam's quiet demeanor and willingness to lead by his actions gained him great respect among his peers. To this day, Liam can't stand to be in a kitchen when anything is being fried." Mrs. O'Connor continues, "The reason I wanted you to come over today was to find out if you knew what was going on with Liam, but also to let you in on some history of our family, perhaps to help you know us better. I can tell you have questions. I could see that, the first time you were here. I want Liam to start living again. He has been alone long enough. If it wasn't for that old dog of his... I don't know!"

"He sure is attached to that dog," says Tina.

"Tina, with Liam, there are reasons for everything. The Irish have a saying, 'If he's not fishing, he's mending his nets.' That means he's someone who is always planning, a thinker. Liam doesn't let a lot of people get close to him. He believes not letting people get close makes it easier when they leave. When his brother James died, was the first time I noticed Liam retreat back into his own private little world."

"He seems well liked by many people," says Tina.

"That is true, true. But I think you can be liked by many, but still feel alone," says Mrs. O'Connor.

"But we were talking about Sandy, weren't we, dear? That dog of his was a present from a high school football player of Liam's. The player was a music student of Kelley's, too. Daniel Edgemont gave Kelley that boxer pup when Liam was recovering from being shot about seven years ago. Liam was hurt pretty bad, and we thought he was going to be medically retired. Liam always said he wanted to complete his shift after thirty years and just retire without any fanfare, but not retire from an injury. Edgemont thought 'Coach O' needed a workout partner. Little did he know, Molley had moved out to start her new career in Atlanta, and Kelley and Liam were now empty nesters. That dog was a welcome addition to the family. Several months passed, and Liam went back to work. Edgemont graduated and went into the Army. He was killed in Iraq several months later. Liam named that dog Sandy because Kelley always called Edgemont 'Sandy,' because of his sandy brown hair. Sandy's been a great companion to Liam, but one day, she'll leave him too."

"Maggie, tell me about the last picture you have of Kelley and Molley," says Tina.

"Are you sure you want to know the story of Liam and Kelley?" says Mrs. O'Connor.

"I'll tell you, but I want you to know, I believe a person can find true love a second time around. God has a plan for us all! Something tells me you and Liam have chemistry. Remember, when God closes one door, He opens another," says Mrs. O'Connor.

"Liam and Kelley were childhood sweethearts. We've known Kelley since she lived across the street from us at age five," says Mrs. O'Connor. "Liam and Kelley were the same age and went to the same schools. On one occasion, Liam, Kelley, and I went down to the shipyards to bring Joseph his lunch. From time to time Joseph would work a second job at the shipyard of his war buddy, Sal Pennilli. We brought him lunch on a warm summer day, and while I was having lunch with Joseph, we heard a loud scream by the edge of the docks. We looked over, and the next thing we saw was Liam jumping into the water. Joseph and I ran over just in time to see Liam pulling Kelley to the side of the docks. Liam and Kelley came out of the water looking like two soaked rats," laughs Mrs. O'Connor. "Kelley had been walking near the edge and fell off the side. Joseph told me later that night, he was proud of Liam. Even at the young age of thirteen, Liam never hesitated to jump in after Kelley. It seemed like they were a couple from then on. We expected to hear about arguments or weekly breakups from the two, but it never happened. They grew with each other through high school and college. Liam was the sports-minded, quiet individual, and Kelley was the red-haired, green-eyed outgoing woman, always busy with her love of music. They respected each other's interests, and at the same time were always very supportive of each other. They loved each other very much. They had chemistry!"

"Maggie, you told me that Molley blames Liam for her mom's death," says Tina.

"Well, Molley just didn't deal with the loss of her mother very well. Molley is an only child, spoiled by all of us her entire childhood. Maybe the worst offender was Liam. Molley was Daddy's little girl while growing up. Whatever that girl wanted, he gave her. She went to private schools all her life, which you may know costs a bit of money. Not an easy task on the salary of a police officer and a public school teacher. You throw in dance lessons, cheerleading camps, formal dances, and of course... college. Kelley and Liam sacrificed for their daughter, like parents do," says Mrs. O'Connor. "We all want to provide better for our kids. Molley is a bright, intelligent, beautiful young woman who is very successful in her career. But I believe Liam and Kelley realized, later in life, that perhaps the greatest gift you provide your children is your time. Molley now lives in Atlanta. She's not married, has had many boyfriends, but when things get serious, the relationship is over. I hope she figures it out for herself soon. I won't be around much longer, and I want to see that child happy. I hope you don't think I'm overly harsh on Molley. It's just as I get older, I don't filter my words as I once did."

"Now Tina, I've been doing all the talking, I want to know more about you! I know how you and Liam met, but why are you really watching his dog?" asks Mrs. O'Connor.

"I don't really know. Chemistry, I guess. I mean, the first time I saw Liam I couldn't keep my eyes off him. I had to leave the room. I did leave the room, but just looked at photos of him in his bedroom while the detectives were talking to him. I can't explain it, really. I was married once. My husband was killed in the first Iraq war. I don't remember ever being this giddy around him," says Tina. "I'm not blind, I can clearly see that Liam loved his wife very much and is in a lot of pain about her death. I've been in his shoes, and it takes time to move on with your life. Now, saying that, I can't deny I have feelings for Liam. I'd like just a chance, that's really what I want, is a chance to see if Liam has feelings for me," says Tina.

"Oh, I think that will happen," says Mrs. O'Connor.

"I sure hope I get a chance," says Tina.

"I can sure see why Liam has opened up to you. You're a beautiful person, both on the inside and out. You speak your mind. I like that very much," says Mrs. O'Connor. "I'm so glad we've had this talk. I have no idea in hell what Liam's up to, but when he returns, there is certainly a *situation*. We'll just call it a situation right now, Tina!"

CHAPTER 9
SHENANIGANS PUB

OH! HOW I'VE MISSED THE WICKED WINTERS of Boston, thinks Liam. The highways are slow, same old Boston. He continues to drive the old Cruiser in the snow up Interstate 95 in a light snowfall. I made good time, 7 p.m., he thinks as he looks down at his watch. It's probably closed. I'll just park outside and jump the fence again, thinks Liam. He drives in the light snow, becoming more and more nervous as he anticipates his conversation. Here at last, thinks Liam. The gate is closed. Shit, okay, I'll just jump the wall like I've done in the past. Liam attempts to jump the eight-foot brick wall and can't grab the top ledge with his right leg. He struggles with both feet scratching at the wall, attempting to grab an edge, until he stops and falls back to the grass. Shit... shit, if T.J. saw that, I'd never live it down, thinks Liam. It's probably the medication I'm taking. Perhaps light beer should be the selection of choice in the future as well. He looks to the end of the wall, about twenty feet away, and notices an open pedestrian gate. He laughs at himself and walks through the open gate, thinking I'm glad it's too dark for anyone to see that. He notices the snow begins to fall through the trees, lightly covering the ground. Perfect. Clean white snow, no imperfections, as it should be. He continues to walk a while through the snow-covered grounds, finally reaching his place of rest.

Beloved Wife, Beloved Husband, Beloved Son. Words crafted into headstones. It just doesn't quite capture each of their life's worth, thinks Liam. Joseph O'Connor, James O'Connor, and Kelley O'Grady O'Connor were the names on the headstones at the St. Joseph Cemetery. Liam had gone to see his heroes and his beloved saint at their final resting place.

I know it's been a while, but I've come to ask something from you all, says Liam as he prays. Dad, you're the strongest man I've ever known. Please provide me the strength to carry this task out, provide me with the strength to see this through. Brother James? I need your courage. The courage it takes to battle, even if the odds are against you. Finally from my saint, my saint of a wife, Kelley, please

158

give me the wisdom to choose the right path, and if it's God's plan for me to join you, may I be in heaven a full half-hour before the devil knows I'm dead. I'll need a good twenty-five minutes with you, and five for a pint! Liam turns and begins to walk back through the cemetery. As he does, he sees the figure of a man walking toward him through the falling snow. He walks toward the man and soon sees it's T.J.

"I thought I'd see you here, Liam. I thought you'd get to town and pay your respects first," says T.J. The two embrace.

"Man, it's good to see you, T.J. I've missed our man dates!" laughs Liam. "I miss whipping your ass in golf, and your wife's cooking. How is Rhonda?"

"She's fine, Liam. She doesn't know you're here. No one does, as far as I know," says T.J.

"I brought that letter I told you about, and a paper from two days ago."

"What's in the paper?" asks Liam.

"There's an article about the death of Nick Torigiani. He was found dead two days ago, across from Shenanigans Pub," says T.J.

The two continue to walk through the cemetery until they exit through the front gate. They walk over to Liam's Cruiser.

"I see you're still driving Dad's old tank," says T.J.

"It's a classic!" says Liam.

T.J. hands Liam the letter from Captain Torigiani and a two-day-old print of *The Boston Herald*.

"T.J., I'm a bit tired and in need of a drink," says Liam.

T.J. asks, "Where are you staying while you're here?"

"I thought I'd stay in Dad's old office above the bar, if Dugan will let me," says Liam.

"Is your mom still part owner of the pub since your dad's passing?" asks T.J.

"Yeah, she's still one-third owner. A silent owner. Big Mac has taken care of the business since Dad died. Mama gets monthly checks from the pub, along with Dad's retirement from the force. That, and the money she got from the sale of their house, she's sitting pretty."

T.J. says, "Liam, I'll follow you to the pub and get you settled. We can talk more then."

"Sounds good." Liam and T.J. drive from St. Joseph's Cemetery to Joseph's pub in South Boston.

The two arrive at Shenanigans Pub, owned and operated for many years by his father and Dugan McSweeney. "Big Mac," as he is referred to, is still part owner and current manager of the pub. Liam and T.J. park in front of the pub and enter through the front doors. Shenanigans has been an established pub in the community for over twenty years. It has, like most well-accepted community pubs, a strong, loyal following of diverse blue-collar Southies.

The pub serves food and drink, so it's commonplace to see neighborhood families within the establishment. Joseph wanted a place that felt like home to all. He believed that serving food and drink was not enough to successfully run a business. He thought people wanted to feel a part of the pub. Dugan and Joseph always tried to remember the names of those who regularly came to the pub, the repeat offenders. The two had the gift of gab, which helped create the open and friendly atmosphere. He remembers his mother's response when his father wanted to buy into Shenanigans: "Well, finally we might get some return on your years of personal investment."

Liam and T.J. enter the pub and are immediately seen by Dugan McSweeney. Dugan stops his conversation with a local patron, walks over to Liam and gives him a hug. Liam, a tall man standing six foot three, is overshadowed by Big Mac's enormous frame. Weighing 365 pounds and standing six foot seven, Big Mac is a gentle giant. He had worked for many years as a butcher in Dorchester.

Joseph and Dugan had become friends years back, after Dugan's shop had been robbed. Joseph was able to locate the suspects and recover Dugan's stolen money. A friendship was struck, and better cuts of meat and poultry were eaten at the O'Connor residence from that time on.

"Liam, it's sure good to see you. T.J., where have you been keeping yourself? It's been months since you and Rhonda have been in," says Dugan. "How is your mother, Liam?"

162

"She's fine. Mean and feisty as ever."

"Drinks for you two? The regulars?" asks Dugan.

"Sounds good," replies T.J.

"Come, sit down, get me caught up with you two," says Dugan. "Feels like old times."

The three men move to a booth in the corner of the pub, down from the noise and activity of the bar. Drinks are brought to the table, a shot of Jameson and a pint of Guinness for T.J.

"Did you get proper authorization for that pint from Rhonda?" laughs Liam. "I thought you only drank wine now, T.J."

"I'm sorry, did you want wine?" asks Dugan, "You did drink Guinness. I just thought..."

"No, this is good, this is fine."

"I'm glad to see you've grown a pair again, T.J.," laughs Liam.

Dugan and T.J. laugh as T.J. shakes his head and smiles.

"T.J., you're one lucky man to have Rhonda. You sure married up," says Liam.

They all laugh, and Liam drinks his Jameson. He grimaces as the whiskey goes down his throat.

"Shit, that's like a torchlight procession going down the throat," he says as the others laugh.

"It's been a while since I've had whiskey."

Liam soothes the burn with a large drink of Guinness.

"Big Mac, I need a favor from you," says Liam. "Could I stay in the office above the pub for a few days?"

"No problem, Liam, the place is just like your father had it. There's a bed and a shower up there. Use it as long as you need it," says Dugan.

Dugan is called away from the table.

"Liam, you could stay with me!"

"Thanks, T.J., but I don't want to bring trouble to your house. This way I'm in a public place, which can make things more difficult."

"Difficult for who?" asks T.J.

"I don't know yet, but I will... soon," says Liam.

He looks down at the newspaper T.J. brought him, and the letter from Captain Torigiani.

"What do you know about Captain Torigiani's arrest?" asks Liam.

"I heard about him when I came on the department, years back. I heard he was doing time in a Federal prison for murder. Whose murder, Liam?" asks T.J.

Both sat back in the booth, each taking a drink from their beers.

Liam says, "I'll tell you what I know, and what Dad told me. You see, Dad and Torigiani were pretty tight in his early years with the department. Uncle Sal made it much easier for an Italian and an Irishman to work together in places like Dorchester, South Boston, really all over Boston. In the '70s and '80s, there were big problems between the Italian family, or the mob, and the Irish mob. But because Dad and Uncle Pennilli were tight, Dad had no problems working the streets as a cop. I wasn't told until many years later that Francis Salvador Pennilli

165

was the head of the Italian mob in Boston. Growing up, I always called him Uncle Sal. My father told me there was no finer soldier than Sal. Through the years, Dad worked from time to time at Pennilli's shipyards. No doubt that Uncle Sal's influence on the streets made it easier for Dad and me to do our jobs. We were able to go places and talk with people who would have never given us the time of day without his nod. To this day, I believe my father's friendship with Pennilli cost him any chance of promotion within the department. Dad never complained and never let his friendship with Sal slip. Uncle Sal's son, Roman, is about my age. He and I would hang out together as kids, but he was never very athletic, and we grew apart. I've heard he has now taken over his father's position, running the streets and the shipyard business in South Boston."

Liam and T.J. drink more from their beers. Liam asks,

"Will Rhonda want to know where you've been tonight? It's ten p.m. already. Will she start calling you?"

"No, I told her I was going to the shooting range at the department, so she knows I'll be gone for a while," replies T.J.

"Torigiani and Dad were partnered up to help defuse some city relations problems between the Italians and Irish during that time. They grew to like each other. About nine or ten years ago, Captain Torigiani was having problems with his teenage son, Chris. He was hanging around with the wrong people and started using meth. When he was about 16 years old, he was caught under the influence and in possession of meth. Captain Torigiani worked a deal with juvenile authorities to defer the sentencing on Chris until he completed a drug rehabilitation program. He completed the program and was sentenced to misdemeanor charges and was placed on probation, timed served. Dad said the boy did fine for a short time, then got back into using drugs his senior year in high school. Chris, while under the influence of methamphetamine, was caught doing a burglary in Charlestown. He was to be tried as an adult, but Captain Torigiani went to the assistant district attorney at that time, Alton Mills, and asked if there was anything that could be done. Mills, a friend of Torigiani's, agreed to put Chris back into a drug program and again defer sentencing."

"You mean he got another second chance?" asks T.J.

"Yep. The kid was a born snake charmer...an extreme bullshit artist," says Liam. "Captain Torigiani just couldn't let him go to jail, which might have been the best thing for him. Chris completed the program and managed to get his GED in the process. He again was placed on probation, with the help of Mills. Mills kept Chris from going to jail. Once out of jail, Chris worked several part-time jobs, but was still running the streets. His father was frustrated with Chris and was tired of dealing with him. He called his probation officer and had him violated for drug possession after Captain Torigiani found meth in Chris's pants. Chris was incarcerated in the South Boston Jail as an adult when Assistant District Attorney Mills got him released into his custody. Mills liked Chris and decided to help Captain Torigiani out by paying to put Chris into a private drug rehabilitation center in upper Massachusetts. He once again successfully completed the program and was released into the custody of Mills. Chris Torigiani was placed on probation, with a promise to the court that he would be living with

Mills until the completion of his probation."

Dugan returns to the table and asks if T.J. and Liam would like another drink, or something to eat. Both men order another Guinness. "Liam, I understand about a kid needing a helping hand or some positive role model to follow, but this sounds wrong," states T.J.

"Well, hold on T.J., it gets worse!" says Liam. "Dad said while on duty, he was called by the communication center and received a special assignment. One not to be broadcast over the police radios. The communication center had him respond to Alton Mills' house on a report of stolen property. Dad said he went to Mills' residence in Charlestown and met with Mills. Mills said Chris had stolen several pieces of jewelry and cash, and wanted Chris located and his items returned. Several hours later, Chris returned back to Mills' house. Mills refused to press charges. Alton Mills was a single man in his mid-fifties, having never married. Neither myself or Dad ever heard Mills talk about current or past girlfriends, ever. Dad said when he returned to Mills' residence to meet with Chris and Mills, there were other men at the house. He told me it looked wrong. He said, 'I have

169

no proof they were poofs or puffers, but it looked wrong, Liam. It looked wrong to me.'"

"Dad told me several months later, Boston police were called again to Mills' house on a peace disturbance call. Chris Torigiani had allowed several friends over, and the gathering got loud and out of control. Alton Mills returned home to find an out-of-control party. Mills called the police and had the individuals removed. Rumors started to spread," said Liam, "within both the police department and the district attorney's office, about an inappropriate relationship between Mills and Chris. These rumors got back to Captain Torigiani. T.J., you can imagine the difficulties Captain Torigiani had dealing with the rumors within the police department. Several months passed, and I'm recovering from being shot when Dad tells me Captain Torigiani was arrested for murder. He told me that Chris Torigiani stole Mills' car and crashed it into a tree somewhere upstate, and was killed. After Chris was buried, Captain Torigiani went to Mills' house, supposedly to retrieve Chris's personal belongings. Something else happened, though, because Captain Torigiani stabbed Alton Mills in the right temple with a six-inch hunting knife. He wrapped Mills' body in a tarp and placed it in the trunk of his car, which was parked in the garage."

"Liam, did Captain T confess to the murder?" asks T.J.

"No, not at first. The body wasn't located for several days after the stabbing. During that period of time, Captain Torigiani worked several shifts at the detention facility. A check-the-welfare call was sent out to daytime patrol officers, and Dad was one of the first responding officers at Mills' residence. He and three others found Mills' body in the garage. All hell broke loose then. He said there were more command staff and officials from the district attorney's office than he'd ever seen before. He told me the Department of Justice was called in to handle the investigation, as it was strongly believed that Captain Torigiani may have been involved. T.J., several days passed and the DOJ arrested Captain Torigiani at work. His fingerprints were found on the knife handle stuck into Mills' head. They also located additional fingerprints on several beer bottles in Mills' kitchen. Captain Torigiani went to trial and stated he believed Mills had lured his son into a homosexual relationship."

"He testified that he looked to the assistant district attorney for help with Chris when he was a juvenile. He admitted to asking for special treatment for Chris to keep him from going to jail. Captain Torigiani said he thought his son would be in danger if put into jail, because cops' kids don't do well in jail. But most of all, Chris was soft. He would have been unable to deal with the harsh environment of county jail. Captain Torigiani was found guilty of voluntary manslaughter and was sentenced to seven years in prison. The jury was very sympathetic toward Captain Torigiani, as it was generally believed that Chris was a pawn, used for pleasure by Alton Mills."

"Liam, why would anyone want to kill Torigiani now?" asks T.J.

"What did the paper say happened?" asks Liam as he looks at the paper T.J. brought him.

"I read the story. It said that his body was found across the street in a parking structure. He had been shot twice in the back of the head," says T.J.

"It goes on to say that he had been released from custody some five days earlier, and he was once a captain with the Boston Police Department." Liam continues to read the paper.

"Why would Captain Torigiani send you a letter?" asks T.J.

"I don't know. I know that Dad went and visited him a couple times through the years. Maybe he's just paying his respects. I'll open this letter upstairs. Let's go," says Liam.

Liam and T.J. leave the booth and make their way over to Dugan McSweeney. Liam asks if it would be okay for him to park his vehicle in the back of the pub where the employees park, where there are outside stairs leading into his father's old office.

"Sure, Liam. I'll unlock the outside door and the office," says Dugan.

Liam drives the Cruiser to the back parking lot, where he is met by T.J. T.J. asks, "Did you even bring any clothes with you? You still have that old bag from Boston College... is that it?"

"Take the bag, T.J. I'm going to get a few things out of the back," says Liam.

Liam removes his handgun and shotgun from the hidden compartment. He takes his bag of golf clubs, shoves the shotgun in the bag, and puts a club head cover over the barrel. Liam says to T.J., "That's my special club."

Liam and T.J. walk up the stairs and into the hallway of the second floor. Liam opens the office door, and they enter the office.

"The place looks the same, doesn't it, T.J.? Big Mac hasn't touched a thing. This sure brings back some old memories," says Liam. "T.J., he's left all the pictures on the walls, just as Dad had them. Pictures of Mama, pictures of Jimmy, and of you and me in high school. Check out the 'fro you had back then!"

They look around at the office, and Liam goes to the bathroom and takes some of his daily medication. TJ asks,

"You still take pills because of your injuries?"

"I take pills because I have no spleen, T.J. Something I'll have do for the rest of my life," says Liam. He doesn't tell T.J. about his Parkinson's disease.

"Let's see what Captain Torigiani has to say."

He opens the letter addressed to him, but sent to T.J.'s house.

"I guess he knew you would be able to get this to me," says Liam. "The letter was sent three days ago, one day prior to his death."

"Read it out loud, Liam," says T.J. "You can't leave me in the dark now...he sent it to my house."

Liam reads the letter to T.J.

Liam, I was very sorry to hear your father passed away several years ago. He was a true friend and a good man. He came several times to visit during my time of incarceration. I'm sure your father told you the reasons that led me to that place. I make no apologies or excuses for my actions, my day of reckoning will come. I was tried, found guilty, and served my sentence as society deemed appropriate. You of all people should know that not everything is as simple as black and white. I've followed your career and was fortunate enough to have your father talk to me about you and the rest of his family. Joseph looked out for mine, while I was unable to. I made a promise to myself that

175

once I was released, I would do all I could to make things right with my family. Since my arrest, my wife divorced me and my daughter hasn't spoken to me.

Two days prior to my arrest, I gave your father a small backpack containing several video tapes. The pack was Chris's. I took it from Mills' house, along with the videos. Liam, please locate that pack and view the videos. Your father said I had dynamite, and whoever possessed it would be in danger. He told me he placed it in a secure location, but never shared that location with me. I know my life's in danger because of those videos. Joseph said he would keep the videos close and guard it with his most precious treasures. I've been to Shenanigans several times trying to get your address, but McSweeney said he didn't know it. He only knows T.J.'s. If you can, and are willing to help me, call Shenanigans and leave a message with McSweeney. He knows where to find me.

Nickolas Torigiani

"Liam, did your dad tell you anything about this?" asks T.J.

"No! He never mentioned videos from Torigiani. All he ever told me was how and why Torigiani was arrested. T.J., whoever killed Torigiani must think I have those videos," says Liam.

"What do you think is on the videos?" asks T.J.

"God only knows. I don't need this shit right now," says Liam.

"T.J., I need to get some sleep. I'm beat. I'll call you in the morning. Are you working tomorrow?"

"Yeah, I work mid-day till 8:00 p.m."

T.J. leaves and Liam lays on the couch, rereading the letter until he falls asleep.

CHAPTER 10

A PICTURE IS WORTH
A THOUSAND WORDS

LIAM SLEEPS FOR A FEW HOURS AND IS AWAKENED by McSweeney, who sees the light on and enters the office. McSweeney looks at Liam and apologizes.

"I thought you were up, because the light was on. I'm closing her up now. I'm going to let you have a spare key to the place so you can come and go, even if I'm not here," says McSweeney as he places a spare key to the pub on Joseph's old desk.

"Dugan, did Captain Torigiani come in here looking for me?" asks Liam.

"Yeah! He wanted to know how to get a hold of you and if I had your cell phone number and your current address. I told him I didn't have anything, but told him T.J. was working for the department now."

"What do you know about his death? I mean, they found his body across the street from the pub," says Liam.

"Torigiani came in here several times over the last week looking for you, and asking others in the pub if they knew where you were living. The word on the street is that he was killed by Pennilli's men."

"Why?" asks Liam.

"No fucking idea," says McSweeney.

McSweeney leaves the office, walks downstairs to lock up, and exits through the back door. Liam looks at the clock on the wall and sees it's 4:00 in the morning. He lays back on the couch and falls asleep thinking about what Captain Torigiani's letter said. He sleeps for a few hours longer and awakes at seven a.m. to snow falling and a cold temperature within the bar. Liam goes to the bathroom and turns on the shower, hoping there is hot water. The shower begins to get hot, so he showers, all the time thinking about the letter and why Uncle Sal would be involved in Torigiani's death.

He completes his shower and takes his daily medication. He retrieves some clothing from his old Boston College bag.

180

Damn, it's cold in here, he thinks while looking for the floor heater. He locates the heater behind his dad's desk near an old china cabinet. Shit! If I open this up, will this fucker start leaking on me? Liam decides to open up the floor heater and take a chance. The heater seems to be working without a problem, just slow to heat up. I never have this problem in Florida, thinks Liam. He looks at the cabinet behind his dad's old desk. He notices an old black-and-white picture of his mother on their wedding day, along with photos of Joseph with Uncle Sal in uniform in Korea. Liam starts to look through the old cabinet and sees more photos of Jimmy in his uniform from Vietnam. He looked so young, thinks Liam. Also in the cabinet, on the upper display shelf, is an encased and folded American flag. Next to the flag is a picture of T.J. and Liam in their high school football uniforms. A picture of T.J. in his Marine blues and a photo of Liam making a tackle against Army. Liam continues to look through the drawers of the cabinet and sees his dad had kept newspaper clippings of Liam's homicide investigations and photos of his promotions. Liam thinks, I never knew Dad even had this stuff up here. He looks at the cabinet and at all the photos and realizes, these are memories that must have meant something to him, his treasures. As soon as Liam looks at the contents as indeed his father's treasures, he continues to rummage through the cabinet, now looking for the video tapes from Torigiani, but finds none. He can't find the tapes even after going through the entire contents of the cabinet. He thinks about Uncle Sal and how it could have been Pennilli's people that came to visit him in Port Saint Lucie.

Liam looks at the cabinet and shakes his head in disbelief. I never knew Dad had this here. I knew he kept some things at home, but never thought here. Liam looks at the encased folded flag and reads the inscription on the case: Presented to the family of Marine Corporal James William O'Connor, killed in action, April 29, 1971, Republic of Vietnam. Liam lifts the case and looks at the faded flag. He thinks back to the day of the telegram and remembers how his mother and father received it. The loss of Jimmy changed the lives of everyone. He starts to place the flag back into the cabinet when he hears a rattle from inside the case. Curious, he opens the case and finds a small envelope containing a key with the number 41 engraved on it. The key indicates that it's from the Rathman Trust Company of Boston. Liam knows that to be a long-standing bank in Boston. The Rathman name is as blue-blood as the Kennedy name. One family went into banking, the other into politics. He knows that's not the bank his father or mother used for their finances when they lived in Boston. He looks at the key and believes it's a key to a safe deposit box. He decides he should make a trip to the Rathman Bank and see who box 41 is leased to.

Liam places the key in his pocket and starts down the stairs when he hears the back door to the pub open. He removes his gun from his waistband beneath his old black leather jacket, and slowly walks downstairs. He looks to the bar area and sees two young women with cleaning supplies. They see Liam and are surprised, as usually no one is in the bar when they clean. Liam tells them that he and Dugan are longtime friends, and that Big Mac is letting him stay in one of the offices above.

One of the ladies says, "You scared me to death. I wish he'd tell us when he's letting someone stay up top. The last guy scared us, too."

Liam asks, "When was the last guy here?"

She says, "Last week there was a guy staying up in one of the offices for a few days, but he left. He too said Dugan told him it was all right for him to stay."

"Do you remember what his name was?" asks Liam.

One of the cleaning ladies responds, "Yeah, his name was Nick. He was a nice guy."

Liam asks if the ladies know what time Dugan gets to the pub. They tell him that Dugan is in by 10:00 a.m. on most weekdays. He asks the ladies how often they clean the pub and offices. They tell him every other day they clean. He asks if they would join him in having some coffee. The three sit for a while and have a cup of coffee that Liam makes from the bar area. He learns that Dugan regularly meets two well-dressed men at the pub every Thursday morning at around 11:00 a.m., just before the bar opens for lunch.

Liam calls T.J. and asks him to meet him at the restaurant across from Rathman Trust Company of Boston in the financial district at 9:30 a.m. He leaves out the back entrance of the bar and drives on the lightly snowed roads to Ruby's, a restaurant across from the Rathman Bank. He starts to park and spots T.J. near the front entrance. He and T.J. enter the restaurant and sit down.

"Have you eaten already?" asks Liam.

"No," says T.J.

They order breakfast, and Liam tells T.J. about the safe deposit box key. He also tells T.J. about Dugan. How Dugan never mentioned that Captain Torigiani was staying at the bar before he was killed. Liam tells T.J. what the two cleaning ladies had told him about the meeting Dugan has every Thursday with two well-dressed men at the pub.

"T.J., first things first. Let's see if this key means anything."

They finish eating breakfast and walk across the street to the Rathman Trust Company of Boston.

Liam and T.J. enter the bank and walk to the front information counter.

"Ma'am?" says Liam. "I have what I believe is a safe deposit key to this bank from my father. I'd like to know who has currently leased this box out."

Liam provides the key, while T.J. shows his Boston Police Department badge. The information specialist tells Liam and T.J.,

"That box is currently leased to a Joseph O'Connor."

"That was my father," says Liam. "He passed away about five years ago. How is that box paid for? Who is paying for the lease on this box?"

"Sir, the box fee is automatically deducted from Mr. O' Connor's monthly retirement check. When Mr. O'Connor started the lease of the box seven years ago, it was fifteen dollars a month, and it has stayed at that rate all these years. Sir, you should really keep the box. It would cost you more than twice that much if you started a new lease now," says the information specialist.

"Is this box a single owner, or did other people have access to the box?" asks Liam.

"Sir, this shows to be a joint tenancy box," she replies.

"Who has access to this box?" asks Liam.

"Our records indicate three total. Joseph O'Connor, Liam Matthew O'Connor, and Nickolas Torigiani."

"When was the last time someone had activity with this box?" asks Liam.

"Our records show since Mr. O'Connor leased the box seven years ago, there has been no activity. No one has accessed the box."

"I have joint tenancy rights to the box, correct?" asks Liam.

"Yes, sir. I'll just need to see your driver's license and Social Security card for proof of identification."

Liam shows his Boston driver's license and Social Security card, and then is led to the area where the safe deposit boxes are located. The information specialist turns Liam and T.J. over to another bank assistant, who states that only the holder of the key can be taken to examine any contents of a safe deposit box. Liam laughs and says,

"Just another way to keep the black man down, T.J."

T.J. flips Liam off, out of sight of the bank assistant, as Liam walks to the area of the safe deposit boxes and is shown to box number 41. The assistant places her key and the key of Liam's into the box, and opens up the container. She then takes the box and escorts Liam to the private viewing room just down the hall. She says,

"If you have any questions or when you're ready to return the box, just pick the phone up in the room, and I'll be back in a moment to escort you out."

She leaves the room, and Liam opens the top of the box and sees three VHS tapes. Each unmarked and in their own separate boxes. Liam removes the tapes from the safe deposit box, gets a small bank bag from the room, and places the tapes in the bag. He picks the phone up and indicates he's finished and is ready to return the box. He is escorted out of the room and back toward the safe deposit boxes. The bank assistant places the box back into space 41 and locks it. Liam meets back up with T.J., and they leave the Rathman Bank.

T.J. asks, "What was in the box, Liam?"

"There are three VHS tapes that my Dad put in the safe deposit box for a reason. He put those tapes there because whatever is on the tapes is trouble... somehow, it's fucking trouble, T.J. I think those tapes are the reason Captain Torigiani was killed, and why I was visited by two hit men. Someone wants these tapes bad," says Liam.

The two walk back to Liam's Cruiser and leave the parking lot. Liam and T.J. drive back to the bar and park in the back parking lot where T.J. left his vehicle.

"T.J., you have to go to work, right? I'll follow you to work and see if I can use the VHS player in the Technical Investigation Unit. Does Jackie still run the audiovisual section?" asks Liam.

"Yes. That girl sure likes you, Liam."

"That was in college, T.J. And besides, she was no match for Kelley," says Liam.

"I think she'll let me use the VHS player and video capture machines. I never had a problem when I was in the department."

Liam follows T.J. to the Boston Police headquarters. Liam makes sure he has his retired identification card and badge in his back pocket before he and T.J. start through the back entrance, Liam carrying the small bag with the VHS tapes under his left arm. T.J. turns to Liam and says,

"Liam, I need to go to the locker room and change before my shift starts."

They enter the police department and start toward the locker room, when many uniformed personnel greet Liam. T.J. walks Liam back to the Technical Investigation Unit, audio-visual section, and Liam looks to see if his old friend Jackie is there. Liam sees Jackie, and she comes to greet him.

"Liam, it's good to see you again. I was so sad to hear about Kelley," says Jackie while giving Liam a hug. "What brings you back here?"

"I'm just visiting T.J. and was hoping I could look at some old VHS tapes of T.J. and me in high school. They are of old football games. Could I look at them on the old VHS player, and maybe use the video capture to take a few still shots? You know us boys, Jackie. Just trying to relive the glory days of our youth," says Liam.

"Sure, Liam. Nobody uses VHS anymore, though. You should just copy them onto a DVD," says Jackie.

"Thanks, I think T.J. wanted his own copy. Maybe I'll just have you help me copy the tapes all to DVDs, if it's not too much of a problem?" asks Liam.

T.J. walks from the Technical Investigation Unit to his assigned duty in the Property Room. Liam says to Jackie, "I'm going to look at the tapes to make sure I've got the right ones first. I may have grabbed the wrong tapes. I'll need your help in a little bit, though. Jackie, you know I'm not a tech guy. Are the machines still in the back room?" asks Liam.

"Yes, Liam you can go back and close the door. No one will bother you. If you need some help, just come and get me, or just put your lips together and blow. I'll hear you. You do know how to whistle, don't you?" asks Jackie.

Liam looks into the eyes of Jackie, smiles and says, "I think I can manage to whistle. I whistled a few times at you in college."

Jackie blushes and looks around to see if any of her personnel heard what Liam said.

"I wish you would have done more than whistle, Liam... that Kelley was a lucky woman," says Jackie.

Liam walks back to the video room and closes the door. He sees the room is positioned so that no one from the outside can see what he's viewing unless they enter the room. Liam locks the door behind him. He sits down and sees the VHS player, and the large screen above the player. He turns the power on to the player and puts a tape in.

The tape begins to play, and it's Chris Torigiani, walking around in what appears to be a very nice residence. Torigiani is talking while walking around the backyard. He is speaking as though he's giving a tour. He says on tape that the house has a large pool, two stories with five bedrooms. He goes on to describe the kitchen and wine room, along with how well the bar is stocked. He walks to the upstairs and enters a bedroom. In the bed of this room is Alton Mills. Mills says to Torigiani, "Put the video down and come to me, my son." Mills is nude. The camera gets moved onto a mount near the foot of the large bed. Torigiani takes his clothes off, and he and Mills perform oral and anal sex on each other. Liam sees this and is not

192

surprised. He continues to view the tapes for forty more minutes before Torigiani gets out of bed and turns the video recorder off, at the request of Mills.

Liam is somewhat perplexed, as it appears that Torigiani is an adult and certainly a willing participant in all the sexual acts. Besides, everyone on the tape is dead. Liam removes the first VHS tape and puts a second tape in. This tape again starts with Chris Torigiani narrating as he is walking around Mills' house. This time a party is occurring. The party consists of Chris with about twenty party-goers, male and female, all around 18 to 25 years of age. He shows several people shooting up what looks to be heroin. Chris walks with the video camera inside the house and shows several of his friends drinking from the bar and walking to and from the upstairs bedrooms. Chris moves from inside the house to the backyard. He records additional party-goers drinking and urinating in the yard. He prompts conversation from several of his guests. Several subjects are smoking methamphetamine and marijuana around a burning fire pit in the backyard. Chris places the video camera down on a table, but leaves it running. The camera captures Chris smoking methamphetamine. Shortly after Chris is finished smoking, he walks to the camera and turns it off. The video is again about fifty minutes in length.

Liam removes the second video from the player and starts to put the third video in the machine when Jackie knocks on the door and asks if he needs anything, or has any questions.

Liam opens the door and asks if the VHS tape conversion to DVD is a high-speed process. Jackie says,

"Yes, Liam. Do you have some tapes you want converted? I'll set the machines up for you, and here are the DVDs."

Jackie prepares the machines to the point that all Liam needs to do is start the VHS high-speed player and turn on the DVD high-speed recorder.

"I think I can handle this, Jackie. Do I owe you anything for the three blank DVDs?" asks Liam.

"I don't want to get you in trouble with anyone."

"You're fine, Liam. I have my own blank DVDs, not the department's. You'll just owe me one!"

194

"Thanks, Jackie."

Liam starts to copy the first tape to DVD. Jackie leaves the room, and Liam locks the door and starts to view the last VHS tape. Like the previous tapes, it's Chris Torigiani narrating while holding the video camera and taping inside Alton Mills' house. This time, Chris walks from the main living room of the house up the stairs, saying on the tape that the party is about to begin. This video shows no one in the house but Chris as he walks up to the second floor. He walks toward an open door of the master bedroom, and the tape begins to pick up several male voices.

Chris walks through the open door and captures several men on the bed, performing various homosexual acts with each other. Liam sees Alton Mills on the video engaged in sodomy with a second older man, whose back is toward the camera. A third, younger man is heard coming into the room from a bathroom adjacent to the bedroom. The third man walks to the side of the bed, and Chris says to him, "If our fathers could see us now, Carmine!" He sees the third nude young man is Carmine Pennilli, the son of Roman Pennilli, Uncle Sal's grandson. This is not good, thinks Liam. Chris places the video on a table at the foot of the bed, but leaves it running. The video shows Chris removing his clothes and joining the three other men. Liam watches the tape and notices the second older man's face. That man changes position, which allows his face to point directly into the camera. Liam recognizes the man to be the current district attorney, Edward Rathman. The four men engage in an orgy of homosexual acts that lasts much longer than Liam cares to watch.

The third film was about forty-five minutes long. Liam removes the film and completes the high-speed recording process on all DVDs. He places the videos back into the bag, takes the three DVDs and puts them in the inside pocket of his leather jacket.

Liam unlocks and opens the door. He sees Jackie, gives her a hug and thanks her for letting him take so much time in the audiovisual room. Jackie asks,

"Did you get what you wanted, Liam?"

Liam tells her,

"I got more than I expected, Jackie. Thank you!"

He leaves the office and walks to the Property Room, where T.J. is working.

CHAPTER 11
BAD FOR BUSINESS

LIAM TELLS T.J. THAT HE IS HEADED BACK to the Rathman Trust Company of Boston to place a few DVDs in the safe deposit box. T.J. asks,

"What was on the tapes, Liam?"

"It's frigging bad, T.J., not good! The tapes are the reason I had two little friends come to pay me a visit in Florida, and probably what got Captain Torigiani killed. T.J., the best place for you right now is here. If you can meet me back at the pub when you're off work, I'll explain everything then," says Liam.

T.J. walks Liam out the back door of the police department and tells him to be careful.

"If it's as bad as you say, you're in danger," says T.J.

"You're right, T.J., but you know the best defense is a good offense. I'm going hunting now."

Liam gets into his Cruiser and starts the drive back to the Rathman Bank.

Liam thinks to himself that both Pennilli and Rathman had reasons to want Torigiani dead, but Pennilli has the means. He continues to drive across town. He parks his vehicle across from the Rathman Bank and starts to walk back into the bank when he notices a vehicle pull into the parking lot. He sees it's two of Roman Pennilli's soldiers sitting in a car, watching him. Liam continues back into the bank and places the three DVDs in the safe deposit box. Prior to leaving, he places the key to the box in an envelope and drops it into a mailbox just outside the bank's entrance. Liam mails the key to safe deposit box 41 to T.J. He walks toward the parking lot with the three videos in a small bag under his hand and his gun in his back waistband. He drives back to Shenanigans Pub.

He parks at the rear of the business and enters through the back door. It's 4 p.m., and there are several customers in the bar.

He walks upstairs, looks out the top window and sees Pennilli's men drive past the rear parking lot. He places the bag of videos on his dad's old desk. He expects that Dugan McSweeney will soon visit him. Liam waits for Big Mac. An hour passes, and Liam hears footsteps coming up the stairs to the office area. Liam removes his gun from his waistband and places it near his Boston College bag behind the desk. Dugan enters the office and asks how Liam's doing today. Liam tells him he's doing fine, and sees that Dugan is looking around the office area and spots the small bag with the videos. Liam walks over to his golf clubs, removes a putter and starts to practice the stroke of putting. He looks at McSweeney and says,

"Dugan, what did Pennilli give you for giving up Torigiani?"

Dugan looks at Liam and says nothing. He is surprised at what Liam knows. Liam takes the putter and swings it, striking Dugan in the right inner knee. Dugan drops to the ground on one leg, and Liam punches him with all of his strength, striking Dugan on the left side of his face. He continues to punch Dugan with both his left and right fists, until Dugan falls.

Dugan grabs the desk and pulls himself back up. Liam says, "What did Pennilli give you for giving up my home address, you fat fuck!"

Liam hits Dugan once more across the nose, at which time Dugan swings and hits Liam in the left ribcage. Liam takes the blow and momentarily loses his breath. Liam takes the putter and hits Dugan in his chest, he drops to the floor. He starts to push himself up, and Liam hits him with a sharp right punch that puts Dugan back on the floor.

Liam yells at Dugan, "How could you do this, after all my old man did for you!"

"I did it for your mother," says McSweeney.

Liam looks at Dugan lying on the floor and says,

"You've got one minute to explain yourself, and if I don't like what I hear, I'm going to walk all over your face."

Liam stands back from Dugan, and Dugan catches his breath and wipes blood from his mouth and nose. McSweeney tells Liam that Salvador Pennilli is the other silent owner in the pub, and that he always has been.

Dugan says that the pub was Joseph's dream, but Pennilli had the money and influence that was needed to be able to operate. He said it was a good thing when Liam's dad was alive and Salvador Pennilli was running the Mob in Boston. Dugan said Joseph never had to work with Sal's son since he took over as the boss in Boston... that it ain't always easy. When Torigiani showed up after getting out of prison, Roman thought he had some videos that could prove to be embarrassing to the family name.

"Liam," says Dugan, "Pennilli told me he'd take the bar if I didn't let him know when Torigiani came in. He figured Torigiani would come to the bar looking for you. Pennilli thought Captain T had the videos at first, but when Torigiani came in here looking for you, wanting to know your address, he thought you had the tapes."

"Dugan, who comes to the bar every Thursday at around 11 a.m.?" asks Liam.

"Pennilli's lieutenants come and pick up their cut of the weekly profits. That's all I know. I didn't see who shot Torigiani. Look, I made the call that he was here, but I don't know how they got your home address. I don't know it," says Dugan.

A waitress from downstairs walks into the office, looking surprised. She said they could hear sounds of a fight and just wanted to check if everything was okay. Dugan McSweeney looks at Liam and asks,

"Is everything okay?"

Liam says, "Yeah."

The waitress leaves, and Liam walks over to his bag, grabs his gun and puts it back into his waistband. He looks down at Dugan, saying,

"You fuck me again, and I'll kill you!" Liam puts his hand out and helps Dugan to his feet. Dugan uses the bathroom to clean himself up. He limps downstairs, back to the bar.

Liam looks at his left hand and sees that it's shaking again. He removes his daily meds from his bag and takes his pills. He thinks to himself, Dugan hits like a mule. Liam is sure he has some broken or cracked ribs. He's starting to feel more and more pain as the adrenaline wears off.

Liam knows it's only a matter of time before Pennilli's men make their move.

He walks downstairs and uses the pay phone in the pub.

"Hello, Roman. Yeah, it's me. Don't you think it's time to end this? Yes, I've got the tapes. Interesting cast of characters. Not really my type of home movies, but hey, I'm sure a lot of people would find it interesting viewing. I know it... I'll be there at 9 p.m. Just you and me, right?"

Liam knows that Roman would never show up at a meeting alone, especially a meeting with Liam. Roman wants to meet at the shipyard, a place Liam is very familiar with. All the times he went to the Pennillis' shipyard to visit Uncle Sal and his dad as a kid, he never remembers Roman ever being there. Liam knows Roman will be covered by his men, and once he gets the videos, Liam's life is in danger. Liam calls T.J. and tells him he'll need his help with something later tonight. He asks T.J. if he could come to the pub, and bring his sniper rifle and plenty of ammunition.

T.J. leaves work early, drives to his house and retrieves his rifle, ammo, and several other items he keeps locked in a gun cabinet. Liam knows that T.J. has some skills that may be needed. He was a Marine who served in the Panama War in the 4th Expeditionary Brigade as a sniper. Liam hopes the old saying about a Marine still holds true: "Once a Marine, always a Marine."

He sits in the office above the pub, looking at the clock. He sees it's 6:30 p.m. and he decides to walk down to the pub and have a drink and a bite to eat. He orders a pint of Guinness and a cold ham and cheese sandwich. He looks behind the bar and sees McSweeney serving drinks, limping from one end of the bar to the other. McSweeney looks at Liam, sitting in the booth across from the bar counter, and hangs his head in shame. Liam gets his beer, which he promptly takes a large drink from, and looks to the front door and sees T.J. enter the bar. T.J. walks to the table and sits across from him. Liam gets the waitress' attention and asks T.J. if he wants anything to eat or drink. T.J. says,

"I'll have what you're having."

Liam tells the waitress, "Another sandwich and Guinness for my brother."

She looks at T.J. and at Liam, and smiles. Liam notices that T.J. has come in all black clothes.

"Shit, T.J., I almost didn't see you there," laughs Liam. "It's like looking into darkness."

T.J. tells Liam that he brought the other items with him, and asks Liam what the hell is going on. Liam tells T.J. what he viewed on the tapes and who was on them. He tells T.J. about how Dugan was pressured by Roman Pennilli to give up Torigiani, and how he danced on Dugan's face earlier.

"Dugan is not to be trusted," says Liam. "T.J., it's like Dad always used to say, 'He's fit to mind mice at a crossroad, but no more!'"

Liam and T.J. finish their sandwiches and beer, and walk back upstairs to the office.

Liam explains to T.J. about the meet with Roman and its location. T.J. tells Liam,

"You know he's not coming alone. As soon as he gets the tapes, he'll take you out. You're a liability he can't afford to have."

"That's why you'll be there too, T.J. We need to even the playing field. I thought you could position yourself on top of the ships' crane that borders the docks. That should give you a clear view from above, about a hundred feet or so," says Liam.

"I'll need you to cover my backside. T.J., it's cold out and it has been snowing. It'll make things pretty hard for you to climb. I thought you might leave before me and scout things out, and get into position a good twenty minutes or so before the meet."

T.J. agrees and asks Liam, "Are you prepared to kill Roman? If you do, all hell is going to break loose."

"I got that covered, T.J. If something happens out there and I don't... well, take care of Mama for me," says Liam.

"I got you covered. Just do what you do best and end this tonight," says T.J.

Liam looks at the pictures one more time in his father's office. He stares at the photo of Jimmy and the encased flag. His father, and him in their department dress blues. T.J. and him in their high school football uniforms. Liam scans to a family photo taken the day his father opened up Shenanigans and sees in the photo Uncle Sal, T.J., Kelley, Molley, and his mother and father.

T.J. leaves the pub at 8 p.m. He goes out the back door and makes sure no one is following him. He drives to the shipyards and parks three blocks from Pennilli's business. He takes his rifle case, jacket, and gloves, and begins to scout the shipyard. He notices the business is shut down and the long sliding bay doors running alongside the docks are closed, but the lights are on. He sees no vehicles or people inside Pennilli's business. He positions himself at the highest point on the ship crane that runs alongside the docks. From this spot, there is a clear view of the docks, and of the sliding doors leading into Pennilli's place. His position within the cab of the crane provides both cover and concealment. T.J. opens his case up and removes his sniper rifle, a Marine M-40A1 with a night scope good for a distance of up to 700 meters. T.J. sits and waits as 9 p.m. approaches.

At 8:45 p.m., T.J. sees a dark-colored vehicle drive into the business and park by the large bay doors. The driver and front passenger exit the vehicle, while a third man opens the back door and gets out. He looks through the scope and sees that it's Roman Pennilli and two of his associates. T.J. sees Pennilli instruct one of the men to park the vehicle away from the entrance. Pennilli then opens the large sliding bay door to the shop and turns the shop lights on. After parking the car to the side of the business, the third man returns to the shop. Pennilli lights a cigar and appears to be nervous, as he is pacing from one end of the business to the other. T.J. looks through the scope and sees Pennilli's men checking their handguns. He continues to scan the surroundings for additional threats.

Liam pulls the old Cruiser into Pennilli's shipyard and slowly drives toward the open doors. He looks over at the crane and can't see T.J. He starts to worry, but has faith that T.J. will be there for him. He passes the front entrance, drives a few hundred feet past the business, and notices Pennilli's parked vehicle to the side of the business. Liam parks his vehicle and tucks his Glock semi-auto into the back of his waistband, and makes sure his old black leather jacket covers the bulge of the gun. He grabs a second 16-round magazine and puts it into his jacket. He grabs the small bag containing the three videos, steps from his vehicle and walks slowly to the open doors. Liam walks into the business and sees Pennilli with his two bodyguards. He looks at Roman and says, "I thought I told you to come alone."

"Now, Liam, you never expected me to come here alone, did you? I'm a respected family businessman in this community, but there are some people out here who might want to harm me. They're here to protect you as well," says Roman.

"Oh. Is that what you call it, protecting me? Roman, I appreciate you looking out for me, but I can take care of myself," says Liam.

Roman looks at the bag Liam has in his left hand and asks, "Is that it?"

Roman waves to him to walk with him inside the business. Roman lifts his hand and gestures toward his men to stay near the door as he and Liam continue to walk further into the business and out of T.J.'s sight.

Liam and Roman walk back into the shop area when Liam hears the sound of the automatic sliding bay door begin to close. Roman continues smoking his cigar. The two men stop and look at each other. Liam says, "You made a big mistake sending your associates down to Florida for me."

"Well, I'll tell you, Liam, I thought you might have those tapes. When McSweeney told me Torigiani kept asking about your whereabouts, I figured you got those tapes from your dad. You see, I always knew about the tapes, and who and what was on them. I knew Torigiani had those tapes hidden. Before he was arrested, he told me he had taken the tapes from Mills' house. He said I'd be interested in those tapes, and especially who was on them."

"Yeah, I guess you would be interested," says Liam.

"You think I didn't know what my son was, and still is? After Mills' death, I thought it would be best for Carmine to work in the family business in Europe, and that's where he has been the last seven years or so. Turns out his personal sexual habits have opened up a new base of clientele. You know, Liam, I sent Pentecost and Shea to find the tapes, not to kill you. But you shot two of my best men," says Roman. "Liam, you've made a lot of people angry. Boston's finest, no unsolved murders and all that shit. You and your old man would have been nothing without my family! Who do you think protected you and your old man all those years on the streets, you stupid Irish mick?"

"It's all about the business, isn't it?" says Liam. "Carmine was an embarrassment to the family, a sweet boy, but you used your own son, too. Did you whore your son off to Rathman for business?" asks Liam, "or was Carmine just freelancing?"

"Liam, you don't have a fucking clue! We've been doing business with the Rathman Bank for decades. My father starting running all of his money through the bank back in the '70s. Who would ever suspect the Rathman Bank of Boston of laundering money for the mob?"

"So how does the current district attorney, Edward Rathman, fit into the family business?" asks Liam.

"Rathman was a bonus, a married man with children who happened to be a member of the Rathman family. Some men are killers, some sell drugs, and others like young men. He has proven over the past years to be an asset to our family, and now that he's the current D.A., who knows what we can count on from Mr. Rathman? He provided me your home address, which didn't turn out well for Pentacost and Shea, but his contacts have proved valuable to the family business over the years. I think Rathman has a lot to lose. His family has a lot to lose, if he is exposed," says Roman.

"You know, Roman, I never liked you as kid. You were always the kid who watched from the sidelines, never wanting to get his hands dirty. I learned later in life what your father did. But how he conducted the family business, and how you conduct it, is frigging night and day! Your father earned respect from the organization and the people of Boston because he was a man of his word, and he wouldn't tolerate certain behavior. He operated with class," says Liam.

"Well, Liam, I'm the boss in Boston now and there's a new way of doing business. I'll take those videos from you now," says Roman.

"Bad for business...tell me, does your father know about this and his grandson?" asks Liam.

"My old man eats his pasta and plays Bocce ball all day," says Roman.

Liam hands the videos over to Roman. Roman looks at Liam and says,

"You think I won't kill you, Liam?"

"No, I don't. I think you would have someone do it for you. You're not the type of guy who would get his hands dirty. Do you think I'm the type of guy who would just let you have the tapes? I'm a threat to a lot of people's business as long as I'm alive. Those tapes are the reason three people already lost their lives. Do you think if those tapes were exposed to the media, you and your mob family could survive? I bet not," says Liam. "Now just maybe, I've made copies of those tapes and have them ready to be sent to various news sources. You see, one of the benefits of working with the Boston Police Department is all the media contacts I made through the years. Not to mention the contacts within the FBI. You see, Roman, you're right. It's all about business.

Do you think it makes better sense for the mob to let you live or die, if this comes out?" asks Liam.

"I just want two things from you, and you'll never hear from me again."

Roman continues to smoke his cigar, but has become increasingly angry at Liam.

"What is it, Liam?" he asks.

"First, the pub goes free. Your interest becomes T.J.'s, no more shakedowns," says Liam. "Second, my family and I live a long and peaceful life. I so much as see a rabid squirrel look at me or my family wrong, I swear to God, I'll drop a dime on you and make the Rathman-Pennilli family video the most viewed film of the year. For these considerations, you'll have my word that I'll never release my copies," says Liam.

Once the bay door closed, T.J.'s line of sight disappeared. T.J. made his way down the crane and to the back door of the business. He entered through an unlocked back door and positioned himself about two hundred feet from where Liam and Roman are talking.

T.J. looks at the bay door and sees Roman's men standing at the front. He sees lights from a second vehicle that pulls up outside the business. He hears the car door shut and a side door open next to the front bay door. Roman's men immediately walk toward the door, but stop when they see it's Salvador Pennilli.

Liam and Roman walk over toward Salvador.

"Uncle Sal, it's nice to see you again," says Liam as he reaches Sal and gives him a hug.

"Pop, what are you doing here?" asks Roman.

"I heard you two were conducting some business tonight, and I thought I might come and see my two favorite boys," says Sal "You see, Roman, you may be the boss of the family now, but I still hear about every move you make and why. When you sent your men down to Liam's place and they ended up in the county morgue, I knew then it was only time before you brought trouble to our family."

"Pop, I can handle it... I can handle Liam," says Roman.

"Uncle Sal, we've reached an agreement, Roman and I. We were just discussing the terms of that agreement before you got here," says Liam.

He looks at Roman, and they both look at Sal.

"Okay, Liam...agreed," says Roman.

Liam reaches out his hand and says,

"You have my word."

Roman shakes his hand, and the two walk over to where Sal is standing. Roman says to Liam,

"It's all about the business, but you're wrong about me, Liam. Who do you think put Torigiani down? You see, the bastard just wouldn't tell us where the tapes were. Turns out he didn't know," laughs Roman.

T.J. listens to the conversation from the back of the business and thinks to himself, Liam, just walk away, walk away. You got what you came for, just walk away. Shit! Shit, don't say anything.

Liam looks at Roman. "Roman, why is it every time I'm around you, I feel the need to check the bottom of my shoes for shit?" Liam looks over at Sal and says, "Uncle Sal, I believe the best part of your son must have been left on the sheets."

Roman's men begin to walk toward Liam, until Roman waves them off.

"Liam, your father was a leach on my father's ass for so many years. And you, you're just another stupid Irish mick who calls a nigger his brother. You and I could have done so much more if we would have worked together," says Roman.

218

T.J. listens, thinking to himself, Liam, just walk away! Just walk and we're done. Good to go. But you're not going to do it, are you?

Sal steps toward Roman and tells him to stop, when Roman looks at his father and says,

"I'm your son, not him!"

"Okay. Roman, seems like tonight you want to get your hands dirty. You want a piece of me? Let's go. Just you and me, here, right now! Whatever happens, our deal still stands. This is just personal. Business is business," says Liam.

T.J. thinks, you just couldn't walk away, could you? No, not Liam. This is not good!

Liam removes his jacket and puts it on a workbench near one of the boats. He removes his gun from his waistband and places it on the workbench. Roman takes his jacket off and puts it near Liam's. While the two men are removing their jackets, Roman's men walk closer, near where the fight will take place. Sal says,

"I don't advise either of you to do this. You both should just walk away from each other."

Both men continue to ready themselves before fighting. Liam looks at Sal and says,

"Sal maybe this should have happened years ago. Things may have turned out differently for the two of us if we had."

"You're right. This has been a long time coming," says Sal.

"All right, then, you might as well call T.J. to come in. Let's have all parties present. I like to know where everyone stands, everyone where I can see them. That way no one takes matters into their own hands," says Sal. "I know T.J. can't be far away. Why don't you call him in, Liam?" asks Sal.

"All right," says Liam.

"T.J.," he yells. "Come in... come to my location."

Liam looks to the bay door and the docks, expecting T.J. to come in from that direction.

"It could be a bit," says Liam.

T.J. silently walks with his rifle in his hand from the back of the business to the front. T.J. gets about thirty feet away when he is finally seen by everyone. Roman and his men seem surprised, but Sal just has a slight smile. He looks at T.J. and says nothing. T.J. positions himself across from Roman's men. He's locked and loaded, and has his handgun concealed underneath his jacket.

"Well, Liam, do you have anything left? I heard you tangled with McSweeney earlier," says Roman.

"I think I have enough for you, Roman," replies Liam.

The two combatants square off toward each other and begin to circle one another, as fighters do. Roman turns and kicks Liam in the left upper chest with a sharp, snapping kick that surprises Liam. He takes the kick and feels the pain from both the kick and the previous shot to the ribs by McSweeney. Liam, six foot three and 210 pound, looks over at Roman, who is six foot, 195 pounds, and is surprised this soft mobster has a little fight.

Roman looks at Liam and says, "Ten years at a private dojo learning Uechi-Rye hardens your body."

He spins and hits Liam across the face, bloodying his lip, slides to the side and

221

sweeps Liam's legs out from under him by kicking his ankles. Liam drops to the ground, making a loud thud sound. T.J. looks on and shakes his head, while still holding his rifle. Liam gets back to his feet while Roman moves from side to side, shuffling his feet, almost taunting Liam by his precision strikes and speed. Liam throws a right punch, only to miss as Roman counters with a blow to the center of his chest. Liam falls back and has his breath knocked out of him for several seconds.

He sees Roman coming forward, and he turns and strikes Roman across his left jaw with a forearm/elbow strike, causing Roman to spin away from him. Roman is dazed, and his nose is broken and bleeding. He looks at Liam and continues to fight. He is no longer shuffling from side to side with the energy he once had, but now seems determined to conclude this fight in rapid time. Both men standing in front of each other begin to once again circle, waiting for each other's next strike. Roman kicks Liam with a spinning back kick with his left leg, that hits Liam in his left ear, causing him to drop to the ground as Roman throws two quick punches to Liam's head.

Liam receives the punches and then moves to the side of Roman, expecting Roman to kick him again. He looks and sees Roman spin his hips to position himself for another leg kick. Roman kicks at Liam with his right leg, but Liam traps the leg and immediately forces Roman backwards, making him hop on his left leg. Liam closes ground toward Roman and again hits Roman with a right forearm to the face. He follows up by tripping Roman to the ground, and continues striking Roman's face and ribs. Roman grabs Liam and tries to grapple with him on the ground. Liam throws additional right punches that hit Roman in his left and right ears.

Roman breaks free from the ground and moves away from Liam. Both men are tired, bloodied, and surprised at each other's abilities. Both square off at each other again, but with little side-to-side movement, as both men are breathing heavily.

Roman's men, Sal, and T.J. are looking on. T.J. looks at Liam and smiles, knowing Liam has fought like this before and won't quit unless he's knocked out.

Liam looks at Roman, smiles and says, "Thirty years on the streets of Boston trained me!"

Roman throws a punch at Liam, but it lacks the speed and sharpness of his previous punches, and Liam easily blocks the punch and hits Roman with a left and right uppercut that drops Roman to the ground. Roman rolls over, and Liam believes he's finished when Roman pulls a switchblade from his back pocket and opens the blade up. Liam backs up, and Roman comes up off the ground and takes a stance, preparing to slash at Liam. Sal yells at his son to drop the knife and stop the fight, but Roman just keeps advancing toward Liam. Roman takes two slashes at Liam before cutting Liam's right chest. He drops back in pain and sees Roman start to lean forward to cut him again, when he traps Roman's knife hand and forces the knife from his hand, breaking his wrist.

Roman drops to the ground on both knees. Liam strikes Roman one time with a massive right punch that knocks him flat on his back. He straddles Roman while on the ground, striking him several more times with both his left and right fists. Liam reaches back, grabs the knife from the floor and lifts it over his head,

224

and begins a downward thrust into the body of Roman. As Liam starts to move the knife down into the motionless body of Roman, Roman's men start to pull their guns.

T.J. looks over at the two men and just taps his rifle while pointing it in their direction, stopping their movements.

A loud shot is heard, which surprises Liam. Straddling Roman and looking into his bloodied, battered face, Liam wants badly to shove the knife through Roman's chest. Sal yells out, "Liam, he's my son!"

Liam looks over from where the shot rang out and sees Uncle Sal holding Liam's gun, pointing it toward the roof.

Liam looks down at Roman's motionless body, and back over at Sal, and for the first time in the last several minutes feels his rage subside. He throws the knife to the back of the business and stands up. He looks down at Roman, who is unconscious, and over to Sal and says, "You two are so very different."

Sal looks at Liam and says, "You're not! You're just like your old man."

Liam moves toward T.J. and has a difficult time lifting his arms. He starts to feel the knife wound and the many blows afflicted on him by Roman. T.J. sees this and grabs Liam's arm, helping him pick his jacket up. Liam turns to Sal, takes his gun from Sal's hand and says, "I count on the word of a Pennilli that our business is concluded."

Liam and T.J. walk from the shop and outside into the cold weather. Liam looks at T.J. and says, "You thought I was beaten, didn't you?"

"No," says T.J. "I just wondered why it took you so long to beat that ignorant son-of-bitch's ass!" he smiles.

T.J. walks Liam back to the old Cruiser and places him in the driver's seat.

"Are you able to drive back to the pub?" asks T.J.

"No problem," says Liam.

Liam starts the Cruiser, and T.J. gets into the front passenger seat. They drive out of the business and up the block to T.J.'s car. T.J. gets out of the Cruiser and into his car. The two start driving back to Shenanigans. Liam notices he's bleeding badly from the laceration on his chest.

He thinks, this is not good for the golf game.

T.J. arrives at the bar just prior to Liam. Both park to the rear and enter through the back entrance. Liam walks up the stairs, goes to the bathroom and immediately looks at his chest. His chest is bleeding from an eight-inch long laceration. T.J. sees the wound and knows it will require a doctor, but knows Liam will never go to a hospital. T.J. walks downstairs and asks McSweeney if he knows a doctor who will make an emergency house call. Dugan asks what's was going on. T.J. briefly tells him about the fight and how Liam needs a doctor. Dugan says his ex-wife's current husband is a gynecologist. McSweeney calls and gets him to come to the pub. Liam lies on the couch in the upstairs apartment with blood-soaked towels on his chest.

Dr. Kent arrives and is led upstairs to where Liam is laying. He starts to look at Liam's injury, when Liam asks, "Who is this guy?"

"He's a doctor, Liam," says T.J.

Dugan says, "He's married to my ex-wife."

"What kind of doctor are you?" asks Liam.

227

"I'm a gynecologist."

Liam just looks at Dr. Kent and T.J., and says, "Be gentle with me, Doc."

Dr. Kent tells Liam he was lucky, because it appears only soft tissue was lacerated. He tells Liam, T.J., and Dugan there appears to be no nerve or major vascular damage. He prepares Liam for stitches by numbing several areas around the laceration. Dr. Kent stitches Liam's chest up over the next forty minutes. Forty-one stitches later, Liam's chest is closed up and a gauze bandage applied. Once his chest stops bleeding, Liam takes a cold washcloth and cleans his bloodied face. He turns to Dr. Kent, T.J. and Dugan, and says, "I feel like I just gave birth. First drinks are on me."

T.J. just shakes his head. Dugan escorts Dr. Kent from the pub and thanks him for his services. He tries to pay him, but the doctor refuses payment and takes a rain check on the drink. Liam and T.J. return downstairs to the bar and sit in a booth across from the counter. Dugan walks back into the bar and comes over to T.J. and Liam, and asks, "Drinks, anyone?"

Liam looks at T.J. and says, "How about a couple pints of Guinness, Dugan?"

Dugan leaves to retrieve the beer, and Liam notices he's still limping. He laughs, and then cringes in pain, as his ribs are hurting when he laughs or moves. T.J. looks at Liam and says, "You didn't have to let me in on the pub, Liam, but thank you."

"Oh, you heard that? I didn't know if you were inside or outside the shop," says Liam. "So you heard everything, then." Liam just looks at T.J. and smiles. "It's good this way. Maybe some soul food is what this place needs."

McSweeney brings the drinks, and he looks at Liam and says, "I'm glad you're okay," and walks from the booth.

T.J. and Liam drink from their beers and Liam says, "I'm a little tired tonight, T.J. It might just be one or two beers."

T.J. says, "It's okay, Liam, no problem."

They continue to drink when Liam turns to T.J. and says, "Have I told you about this woman I met in Port Saint Lucie?"

T.J. looks surprised, as this is the first time Liam has ever talked about a woman since Kelley's death.

"There's something about her that gets under my skin a little. Can't explain it, really," says Liam.

T.J. looks at Liam with a big smile and says, "Tell me about her. No, let me guess. She has dark hair and big boobs, right?"

He looks at T.J. and says, "Well."

"I knew it," says T.J. "You're a boob man. Liam, all the years I've known you, you like tall, dark-haired women with big boobs."

"T.J., what can I say? It gets cold in Boston. I need to be properly warmed up at night," smiles Liam.

"Good for you, Liam, good for you! You deserve to be happy. You're a good man."

"T.J., these past several days I've felt more alive, more driven, and more useful than I've felt for months," says Liam.

"You have always been driven to succeed. That's how I knew you weren't going to be beaten by Roman. I knew as long as you were conscious, you would continue to fight. There's no quit in you. That's why I was surprised when you retired and moved from Boston after Kelley's death. It was like you just gave up living, like you just quit on yourself," says T.J.

Liam and T.J. order another beer and drink into the early morning hours before Liam walks upstairs and goes to bed for the night.

CHAPTER 12

RESURRECTION OF A LONELY MAN

LIAM IS AWAKENED BY PAIN IN HIS CHEST, ribs, face, and many other parts of his body shortly after 10 a.m. He rolls over on the couch to see a note left by T.J. that reads, "I'll be there at 10:30 a.m. to pick you up for breakfast before I have to go to work." Crap, thirty minutes to shit, shower, and shave, thinks Liam. Liam rolls off the couch and remembers he should take his daily meds. He takes his pills and works his way into a shower, carefully working around his bandaged chest. He lets the warm water rejuvenate his achy muscles for several minutes before ending his shower.

Thirty minutes pass, and Liam is ready for his breakfast date. He walks downstairs and sees T.J. talking with Dugan. Dugan looks at Liam and says,

"I heard what you did for T.J. and me with Pennilli. I don't know what to say, except thank you." Dugan puts his hand out for Liam to shake.

Liam pauses and reaches over, and then shakes Dugan's hand and says,

"Keep up the good work. A fine neighborhood pub is all my father ever wanted."

Liam and T.J. leave the bar and go across the street to a Starbucks.

Liam and T.J. place their orders and wait for their coffees. Liam tells T.J. that he'll be leaving for home today. He says,

"Mama expects you to come and visit her soon. Look, the weather in Florida is a bit warmer. You and Rhonda should come down and stay with me awhile. I'll show you the sights. I mean, they've got Guinness there too."

"I'd like that, Liam. Maybe I'll work on my tan," says T.J.

Liam laughs and looks outside, and sees it's raining. The two sit for a few more minutes before they cross the street and go back into the pub. Liam and T.J. start moving Liam's bags from the office and pack the Cruiser.

They return inside. Liam gives the key to the pub to T.J. and thanks Dugan for the use of the office. He turns to both of them and says he'll be back in the summer. Maybe then they can all catch a Red Sox game. He walks out the back door, gets into the Cruiser and looks back to see T.J. at the back door. He drives off, headed to Interstate 95 South.

Liam navigates the highways of Boston and thinks to himself, I feel like shit. Every bone in my body hurts, yet I feel more alive than I have in months. He drives for about three hours before he decides to stop and get gas. He knows he needs some beef jerky and Gatorade. After getting some supplies, he sees a pay phone and decides to make a phone call home.

"Hello, Mama. Yeah, it's Liam. I'm okay, I'm coming home. I'll be home in a day or so. I'm fine... Oh, is that right? T.J. called and told you everything. Well, I'm on my way home, I'll see you soon. I should what? Mama... I know, she's a very nice lady. Okay, I'll call her. I love you too, Mama, goodbye."

Liam just shakes his head, thinking about T.J. calling Mama, T.J. the informant! Liam looks at the pay phone and hesitates to call Tina. He finds himself getting nervous just thinking about calling her. He smiles and dials her cell phone number.

"Hello Tina, it's me, Liam. I'm okay... I'm coming home. It's really good to hear your voice too. How are you doing? I don't know, I'm on the road now, but it'll be a day or so. She is...good, I miss that old dog. Okay, I'll call you again when I'm closer to home. Tina, if you get a chance, can you tell Lieutenant Tibedoe the little matter with the two dead bodies has been taken care of? There won't be any further problems in Port Saint Lucie. Okay, Tina, I'll be safe... I look forward to seeing you too. Goodbye."

Liam continues to drive south toward home, eating his jerky and drinking Gatorade. The energy and drive he had going to Boston seems to be as strong going home. He drives and thinks about Molley, Kelley, Tina, and his mother. My little fab four, thinks Liam. Liam drives for several hours, making gas and coffee stops in several states. He stops in Florence, South Carolina, and has dinner. Liam is having difficulty walking, and his face has bruised up pretty bad. He notices people are looking at him like he's the Elephant Man or something.

He sits and eats his meal and starts to feel tired. He decides to stay the night in Florence, and start back on the road in the morning. He finds a hotel off the freeway and checks in for the night. Once in his room, he looks at his chest injury. There's been some seepage of blood from the stitches, but things seem all right. He sleeps through the night and doesn't wake until 10 a.m. the next morning. An unusual occurrence for Liam—not his normal routine. He is accustomed to waking at 5 a.m. every morning.

Liam gets back on the road at around 11 a.m. and knows he has about eight hours of driving time left. He continues to drive, stopping several more times to get fuel and drink. Just after 8:00 p.m., Liam drives into Port Saint Lucie, where it's dry and the temperature is 65 degrees.

He unloads the old Toyota Land Cruiser and walks to his condo. Mrs. Sandrini is walking her dog in the complex and is surprised to see Liam. She says hello to him, and then notices his facial injuries. She asks if Liam is all right and continues walking her toy poodle. He walks to the front door of his home and opens the door. He steps through the entryway and sees his mother, his daughter, and Tina seated at the table, having chocolate cake together. Sandy is lying on the floor near the ladies and gets up to greet Liam.

Liam looks at the startled ladies and can see them looking at his face. He can't believe what he's seeing. He looks at Molley and wants to say so much to her, but is speechless. He looks over at Tina and smiles, and thinks to himself, "T.J. was right... tall, dark-haired, and big-boobed!" Somehow Liam feels like a little kid who just got caught with his hand in the cookie jar. He begins to feel nervous. He thinks, what have they been talking about?

He walks slowly into the condo, carrying his bags. He walks over to the ladies and hugs his mother first. She stares at his face and notices blood on his shirt. Liam looks over toward Molley and she stands up and hugs him. He then looks over at Tina, who has gotten up from the table. He focuses on Tina and steps closer to her, reaches out and hugs her. She puts her arms around his waist and says nothing as her head lays on his chest.

Tina hugs Liam and has difficulty letting go. She finds herself breathing faster, and the hairs on the back of her neck are tingling again. She tells herself, "just breathe."

Liam releases Tina and steps back from the table. Tina says,

"I thought you were going to call when you got closer."

"We made dinner for you. We thought you might be home earlier," says Molley.

"We had dinner without you and had ourselves a bit of cake and coffee," says Mrs. O'Connor.

"Oh, is that right, Mama? Your special Irish coffee, I bet," says Liam.

"We put the food in your refrigerator. All you had in there was beer anyway, Liam. It was good that Tina bought food to make a meal for us all," says Mrs. O'Connor.

Liam puts his bags into his bedroom and goes back out to the living room, where he answers all the question the ladies have about Roman and Uncle Pennilli. As the evening gets later, Molley says she is staying with her grandmother and is going to drive her home before it gets too late. She says,

"I want to see you again tomorrow sometime, Dad! I'll call you tomorrow."

Molley and Liam's mother leave. Liam and Tina continue to talk for awhile in the front living room. Tina says to Liam,

"Have you been seen by a doctor? You look like you have some broken bones in your face."

"I was seen by a doctor who looked at my injuries and stitched me up. My face and ribs are pretty sore, but I'm feeling better every day."

Tina tells Liam that she has been staying at his place since he left, just to make things easier for Sandy. He says,

"Fine by me. I'm sorry I didn't have any food in the place."

Tina says she has to work in the morning and should get home. Liam looks at Tina and wants her to stay, but feels slow and steady is the best course. He asks Tina if she would like to go and have dinner tomorrow night. She accepts and leans over and hugs Sandy, and tells her to take care of Liam. As she is walking out,

Tina turns and looks back at Liam. He steps toward her and they kiss. He steps back, and Tina looks at him and says,

"I've got to go, but I'll see you tomorrow around 6:00 p.m. or sooner, Liam."

She walks away, and Liam closes his door and thinks, she smells good, too.

Liam makes his way to the couch and watches an old movie with Spencer Tracy and Katharine Hepburn. He lays on the couch and notices it smells like Tina. This could be a long night, he thinks. He falls asleep as the movie continues on. While Liam is sleeping on the couch, Sandy is sleeping in her favorite chair.

Liam awakens the next morning just before 5:00 a.m. He takes a shower and allows the hot water to soothe his aches and pains. He removes the dirty bandage on his chest and sees the stitches are healing fine. He puts some old, comfortable clothes on, goes to the kitchen and makes some coffee. He sits at the kitchen table drinking his coffee, thinking about taking Sandy for a long-awaited walk, when Sandy begins to growl and walks toward the front door. He hears a knock at the front door.

Liam walks over to the door and wonders who could be at his door this early on a Sunday morning. He opens the door and is greeted by Chief Green and Lieutenant Tibedoe of the Port Saint Lucie Police Department. He asks them in and if anyone would like a cup of coffee. They both ask for coffee and apologize for coming to his place so early.

"Liam, would you look at something for us, please?" asks Chief Green.

Lieutenant Tibedoe gives Liam a digital camera and prepares the camera for him to see a series of photos. He's shown the first photo that shows an old box truck parked on the side of the road just outside the city, leading to the Savanna Preserve State Park. Chief Green says one of his patrolmen found the truck there last night.

"The truck was stolen out of Miami four days ago," says Lieutenant Tibedoe.

Tibedoe brings up the next picture on the digital camera that shows the back doors to the box truck opened and what appears to be three young women in their late teens or early twenties, all hanging from the roof of the box truck.

Lieutenant Tibedoe gives the camera to Liam, who scrolls to the next photo. That photo shows three women bound by military-grade parachute det cord around their hands and ankles, with all three hung by the neck with a hangman's noose. The cord continues up through eye-bolts attached to the roof of the box truck. All the women are nude. He scrolls to the next photo and sees that the women appear to be Caucasian. Two of the murdered victims have had their breasts cut off by a sharp cutting instrument. All three have been incised from their vaginas to their abdomens. Blood has filled the floor of the truck, and it appears to have dried in most places. The eyes of the women are intact, and all the victims are facing the two back doors of the box truck. Liam scrolls to the next picture, but Lieutenant Tibedoe tells him, "That's enough for now."

Liam asks, "Have you arrested anybody yet?"

Chief Green says, "We have no suspects. We don't have shit! I'm here this morning asking if you would consider working with us as a consultant. I've talked to Deputy Superintendent Finnegan about you. He said you were the best homicide detective Boston ever had. We've never seen anything like this here before. Will you help me—will you help us?"

"Well, Chief, just what haven't you told me?" asks Liam. "Because I'll tell you this much. Whoever did this, has done it before."

Liam pauses, looks at Chief Green and says, "I'll give you an answer tomorrow morning. Is the box truck still out on the road, or have you finished processing the crime scene for evidence and moved the truck?"

"We've completed the processing out on the road, but the crime lab wanted the truck transported to their lab. They plan on completely going through the truck for any evidence, starting tomorrow. The bodies have been taken to the morgue and autopsies are being conducted as we speak. The pathologist probably won't get to all three of the ladies today, so there should be a great deal of additional information tomorrow," says Chief Green.

"That's good to know, Chief," says Liam.

◁○▷

Chief Green and Lieutenant Tibedoe thank Liam for the coffee and leave his home, and begin to walk out toward the parking lot.

"Chief," asks Tibedoe, "do you think he'll help?"

Chief Green looks at Tibedoe and says,

"He's working on the case right now. He's going to view those digital photos in his mind over and over, throughout the day. We sure need him!"

The two get into their vehicle and start back to the Port Saint Lucie Police Department. Once at the department, Chief Green turns to Lieutenant Tibedoe and says,

"John, I'm going to temporarily assign Officer Youngblood to the detective division until this case concludes. We could be in for a long and disturbing investigation. Deputy Chief Finnegan told me Liam O'Connor worked with several FBI profilers throughout his time in homicide at the Boston Police Department. He said by the end of O'Connor's career, he had been successful in profiling several killers, which in turn helped lead to their arrest."

The two return to the city's crime lab. They watch the crime scene technicians and serology experts start the long, methodical process of gathering evidence from the box truck.

———◦◦◦———

Liam closes the front door, walks back to his kitchen and sits at the kitchen counter, thinking about Chief Green's proposal. He sees his left arm start to shake slightly and thinks to himself, this is not going to slow me down. Besides, it's a constant, rhythmic movement, like I'm a human metronome. He walks back to his bathroom and takes his daily medication for Parkinson's. Liam's head is flooded with thoughts. He thinks to himself, I just returned home from one incident in Boston, only to realize I want to live again. I now have feelings for another woman, other than my deceased wife, and I'm not sure how I feel about that. My mind tells me one thing and my heart another. Am I ready to be in a relationship yet? My daughter has reached out to me for the first time in a long while. Is she finally wanting a relationship? Of all the times to be asked to hunt a killer! Kelley always said, "You need to show your daughter your love. She needs your affection. To you, love is a noun. You need to make it a verb and show her." I always hated when she did that schoolteacher shit.

Liam thinks about Chief Green's proposal and keeps thinking of a line from the movie The Godfather. "Just when I thought I was out, they pull me back in!" All kinds of thoughts race through his mind as he walks back to the kitchen. He takes a sip of coffee, looks over at Sandy and says, "It's a fine mess I've got myself into." She barks at him and stares as she sits in her favorite chair in the living room. "Sandy, old girl, I don't think I'm wired to just sit and watch old movies with you all the time. Will you forgive me?" Sandy barks once at Liam. He looks at her and thinks, what a great communicator you are, and cute too. He bends down and hugs her, and says, "You're my girl."

Liam reaches for the leash, and Sandy gets up from the chair and walks toward the front door. He looks at her and says, "You ready for a walk?" He takes her for a walk around the complex. He can't help but see the photos of those murdered women in his head. Each photo pops up over and over in his mind. He thinks, the killer is very organized, neat, and careful. He knows this not from possible evidence collected, but from what was not present in the photos. He's already thinking about the killer or killers and what the photos are telling him. "Homicide scenes will always speak to you, Liam, either by what is left at the scene, or by what is missing." This was something Gordon Zimmer, his old homicide partner, had taught him during their brief time together.

CHAPTER 13

YOU CAN'T TEACH AN OLD DOG NEW TRICKS!

As he walks Sandy around his condo complex, he comes to the conclusion he wants to talk to his mother and daughter about the proposal brought to him by Chief Green. He finishes walking Sandy and calls his mama, Mrs. Maggie O'Hara O'Connor.

"Mama, it's Liam...good, I was wondering if Molley was still there. Would it be okay if I came over in a few minutes to talk with the two of you? Okay...I'll be there around noon. We can have some of your special coffee and lunch. I love you too... I'll see you then, goodbye."

He hangs the phone up and just shakes his head, laughing to himself. She's been having her daily special coffee for over fifty years, and she still doesn't think she drinks hard liquor. He cleans his condo up, gets into the old Land Cruiser and drives to his mother's residence at the Carriage House assisted living facility. As he arrives he looks at the lakes surrounding the property, the fine-cut manicured grass, and the beautiful scenery of the Wanamaker Golf Course, he feels his mother is in a place where she's safe, comfortable, and most of all, happy.

He knocks on the front door of his mother's apartment. The door opens up, and it's Molley. She opens the door, steps forward and gives him a hug. He looks at Molley and tells her,

"You're so beautiful. You were blessed with your mother's beauty."

He walks into his mother's apartment and sees her in the kitchen preparing food. He says,

"What's for lunch, Mama?"

She says, "Fried Spam!"

He looks at his mother and Molley, and they both start laughing. Since Liam was a young boy, he has disliked Spam, but his father loved it.

"Liam, you know your father loved that stuff. He liked it fried or just spread from the can, placed onto crackers or as a Spam-loaf. He learned to like Spam while he was in the Army serving in Korea," says Mama.

"Mama, James and I hated Spam days. All I can say is our dog never went hungry those days, because we gave all of the Spam to the dog," laughs Liam.

Maggie, Molley and Liam sit and have a nice lunch—one of Liam's favorites, chicken primavera with marinara sauce and a cold Guinness. After lunch they all move to the living room, where Mama asks if anyone would like a coffee. Molley looks at her dad and smiles, and Liam tells his mother,

"We're fine, Mama. Besides, if I have one of your coffees, I probably couldn't drive home."

Once Mama returns to the living room with her special Irish coffee, she and Molley ask Liam how he is feeling, and how the stitches in his chest are doing. He tells them he feels fine and his chest is healing.

"I plan on getting the stitches taken out in about a week," says Liam.

"So, Liam, the chief asked if you would help out on a murder investigation, didn't he?"

Liam, surprised, looks at Molley and his mother and says nothing. He just lowers his head.

"Liam, Tina called and spoke with Molley and me about the investigation. She told us that she's been reassigned to a small group of investigators that will be working to find the person or persons responsible for the murders. She told us Chief Green had asked for your help, and is expecting an answer in the morning. She thought you might be at a crossroads about going back to investigating murders, given all that has recently happened. She thought you would need help with your decision. That girl has good instincts. She is truly worried about you, Liam."

"Have you made up your mind about whether you'll help out or not, Dad?" asks Molley.

"Liam, are you looking for some type of absolution from Molley and I? Because you need none of that, son. You can't turn your back on these people and not give them the help they need. Your help could stop more deaths, son," says Mama.

"Dad, I know Mom always understood that, but I didn't. I was kind of a selfish kid. I wanted you to myself," says Molley.

"Molley, that's not your cross to bear. I could have made more of an effort too," says Liam. "You just never saw how I'm wired. I mean, your mother always knew when I was investigating murders. My mind was always thinking about the case at hand. If I was at home, my mind was thinking about the case, reviewing photos, statements, over and over in my head. So even when I was at home with you and your mother, most of the time, my mind was other places. Molley, you never understood why I had to have everything organized at home. Everything in its proper place, neat, clean, straight nothing undone. It's classified now as obsessive compulsive disorder. That affliction helped me in the type of work I did, because I was driven to succeed, driven to be organized with every detail covered. Which helped my work, but it doesn't always fare well in your personal life."

"I know. I have a touch of that, too. It's taken me a while to understand this about you," says Molley.

Liam replies,

"Even now I have insomnia. My mind sometimes works all the time and keeps me from sleeping. When I was in the middle of a murder investigation, it was common for me to only sleep a few hours a night."

"You see, Molley, your mother took Liam for who he was and still is. Sometimes she never got all of his attention when he was with her, and sometimes she did, but she always loved him. She was proud to say, I'm Mrs. Liam O'Connor," says Mama.

"Liam, what are you going to tell the chief?"

"I don't know, Mama. I want to talk with Tina first," says Liam.

"Oh, don't be mad at her, Dad. She really is concerned about you," says Molley.

"I've got so many thoughts when I'm with Tina...like I'm being unfaithful. I have feelings for Tina. I mean, we haven't done anything. You know what I mean," says

Liam, looking toward Molley and his mother.

"Liam, you listen to your heart," says Mama.

"I've got a lot of ghosts in my mind that I need to set free," says Liam.

"Dad, we know how you feel toward Mom. You will always love her. When you're ready for a relationship again, we are one hundred percent behind you. We want you to be happy. You deserve to be happy," says Molley.

"Everyone needs to be happy, Molley, or we'd have a world of people like Uncle Henry, the grouch!" laughs Liam.

"Liam, I like Tina. I just wanted you to know that," says Mama.

"Okay, ladies, I need to go and take care of some things. I enjoyed having lunch with my two favorite women. Molley, how long will you be staying with us?"

"I'm staying with Grandma for the next few days, before I have to go back home."

"I'll call you guys later tonight," says Liam.

"Liam, don't you forget, you have a date with Tina tonight," says Mama.

Liam says, looking surprised,

"You guys seem to know everything about my P's and Q's."

He starts to open the door to leave when his mother says,

"You'd better take that girl someplace nice tonight."

He walks out of the Carriage House, shaking his head in amazement at how the three amigas have begun to work together. Liam mumbles to himself, "I'll take her someplace nice, someplace fun, something low stress for us both. I'll just see if she and I see eye to eye on things. I don't care if she is beautiful, dark-haired, big-busted. There are other, deeper issues than just physical attraction... well, that's my story, and I'm sticking to it!" Liam gets into the old Cruiser in the parking lot of the Carriage House and calls Tina on his cell phone.

"Hello, Tina, it's Liam... I'm fine... it's nice to hear your voice too. Okay, you plan on being at my place at six tonight. Yes, we're going out... no, you can dress casual... I look forward to seeing you then as well. Bye."

Liam ends the phone call and thinks to himself, that went just like I thought it would. She played me like a fine-tuned violin. My friend, you could be in trouble! Those ladies might be too much for me.

Liam returns home and prepares for his date with Tina, when he receives a phone call from T.J.

"Hello T.J. How are you? I'm doing good...yeah, my chest is healing fine. How's the bar business coming along? Molley called you and told you! I don't know what I'm going to do yet. Right now, I'm getting nervous about a date I have with Tina tonight. How is your lovely wife Rhonda and your kids doing? Good... I'm glad they like the bar, too. I don't know, T.J., every time I investigate a homicide it takes something out of me. This one looks bad. It's going to be a long hunt, unless we get lucky somehow. Yeah, three ladies butchered and hung, dressed out like deer. I know... I know, T.J. That's what Mama said. Thanks, I'll need it. I'm taking her to my favorite place in Port Saint Lucie in March. Why not? Well, we'll just see if we're compatible, then. There's nothing wrong with that place! Okay, I'll be good. Goodbye."

Sandy growls and looks at the front door just before the doorbell rings. Liam makes his way from his bathroom. He opens the door and sees it's Tina.

"Come in. Let me get my keys and turn some lights on before we go."

She walks inside. He looks at what she's wearing and how her clothes accentuate the curves of her body as she walks past him. He smells the perfume that has haunted him the last few days. He looks at Tina, stares into her eyes and smiles. Tina looks at him and says,

"I was just trying to help you... I hope you're not mad. I called your mom and told her about Chief Green's proposal."

"I know, Tina. It's fine, I understand."

He just stares at Tina for a few seconds before he turns a few lights on and escorts her back out the front door. He walks her to the parking lot and opens the door to the Land Cruiser. She looks at his car and says,

"We can take my car instead."

Liam stops at the front passenger door, opens the door and puts his arm around her waist.

"Now, Tina, never judge a book by its cover. This... old truck has a lot of life left in it."

She smiles and steps up into the Cruiser. He makes his way around to the driver's side and enters. He takes a deep breath and smells Tina's perfume, and once again looks at her long brown hair that harbors the natural beauty of her face. He recalls what his father once told him. "Don't be fooled with garb and glamour, the proof is in the pudding. Take the makeup off and remove the clothes. If she makes you quiver where you stand, you've got a keeper."

He drives from his place and starts to his destination for dinner. During the drive, she says,

"I heard about what Chief Green asked you. There's been a small group of detectives assigned to this case, and I've been reassigned to this case as well. Do you know what you're going to tell the Chief?"

Liam replies,

"I don't know, Tina. I've got to get a few things straight in my head first."

He stops the car and says to Tina,

"Okay, we're here."

She looks around and sees they're in the parking lot of the Port Saint Lucie Mets baseball stadium.

"This is it?" asks Tina.

"Yeah, it's Thirsty Thursday. You get two beers and two dogs for five bucks," says Liam.

"It's spring training, so we're likely to see anyone play tonight."

Tina, looking surprised, gets out of the vehicle and walks with Liam through the turnstiles. They go over to the concession stands.

"How many would you like, ma'am?" asks Liam.

"Is it a foot-long?" she asks.

He looks at Tina, smiles, and just shakes his head. Tina, realizing the double meaning of her question, looks at him and says,

260

"I've got high standards."

"I don't think you'll be disappointed," says Liam.

He orders two dogs and two beers for the two of them. He gets the food and they walk to their seats behind third base, several rows up. They settle into their seats.

"Do you come to the Mets games often?" she asks.

"I like spring training baseball. You see lots of players from different levels. Some players working themselves up the organization, and some working themselves down. For me, I like to come here and think about things, drink some beers and watch the kids run the bases between innings."

Tina and Liam continue to eat their hot dogs, drink beer and watch baseball for the next hour.

"Liam, you're right. I like watching the young kids run the bases, trying to beat the mascot. They're so cute!" says Tina.

CHAPTER 14
TWO BURGER SAM

"LIAM, DID YOU EVER HAVE A WOMAN PARTNER when you worked homicide in Boston?" asks Tina.

"Yes I did. One woman partner. Detective Samantha Masters—Sam. Sam and I worked together for a little less than a year before she was transferred to Internal Affairs. She was a hard worker, always trying to prove herself around us. Prove that she belonged in the homicide unit. Finally, we had 'the talk,' and things got straightened out."

"What did you mean, 'the talk?'" asks Tina.

"Well, almost every partner I've had, there was a period of adjustment we both went through, man or woman. I would usually sit down and explain how I think, how I work, what my pet peeves were, like you would do with any relationship that's just getting started. My partners would let me know what to expect from them, and we just worked from there. Some of my 'talks' with partners were more confrontational than others, but it always worked out. Sam and I had fun for the brief period of time we worked together. I gave her the nickname 'Two Burger Sam.'"

"Why'd you call her that?" asks Tina.

"She earned it, after a homicide case we worked."

As Liam and Tina sit and watch the Saint Lucie Mets play, he tells Tina about the case.

—◦◦◦—

"Liam, Sam, get your sorry asses in my office," yells Lieutenant Mahoney.

Sam looks at Liam and asks,

"Does he always yell at everyone like that?"

Liam and Sam get up from their desks and start walking toward the lieutenant's office.

"He treats everybody like that. He speaks like that to everyone. He's a human resource manager's nightmare, but I think he's a good and fair supervisor, Sam," says Liam. "I was a little thrown off at first, too, when I was just starting out here."

Liam and Sam walk into the lieutenant's office.

"Shut the damn door, Liam," says the lieutenant.

Liam reaches back, shuts the door and smiles at Sam.

"We've got a homicide in a motel in the Jamaica Plains neighborhood. I need you and Sam to handle it. What I know from the on-scene supervisor is that one person is dead at The Beacon Motel. Liam, you take the lead and keep me posted on what the hell is going on. You know the brass will be on me like flies on shit," says Lieutenant Mahoney.

They walk out of the lieutenant's office, and Liam just smiles.

"Sam, I've been in this unit for five years. That's his normal, loving self."

They leave headquarters and drive to The Beacon Motel. Just as the two step away from their unmarked detective vehicle, Sam asks,

"Liam, why is it you always drive?"

"Just an old habit, I guess. Do you drink whiskey, Sam?" asks Liam.

"No, why do you ask?"

He just smiles and walks toward the motel with Sam. The yellow crime scene tape is stretched across the front door of room 12, on the ground floor of The Beacon Motel. Sam and Liam are met near the front door by Sergeant Patrick, who tells them a woman called 911 at about three that morning. She stated someone had broken into their motel room, shot her friend and took his wallet. Sgt. Patrick said the woman was with an officer at the front office. Liam asks if a crime scene log has been started, and how many individuals have been into the room since the start of the log. Two officers entered since the ambulance personnel declared the individual dead, says Sergeant Patrick. Liam and Sam put disposable gloves on and paper booties on their feet, prior to going into room 12.

Both detectives enter the room. Liam immediately sees there's no other doors leading into the room, other than the front door. The motel doesn't have adjoining doors from one room to another. He notices there is only a single large window near the front door. Lying on the bed is a white male, in his sixties, with a single gunshot wound to the chest. Sam looks at the body and sees that his hands are dirty, and his fingernails are full of black grease. She sees pants on the floor that are dirty and stained, and what appears to her as tobacco stains on his fingernails.

"Looks like our victim liked to smoke a lot," says Sam.

Liam looks over at Sam and the body, and says,

"Did you see a ring on his finger?"

"No, nothing on his fingers and nothing on the nightstand," says Sam.

She notices Liam looking at the door, and the lock and its striker plate.

"Sam, there's no sign of forced entry. I mean, you have to manually lock the door yourself by turning the deadbolt closed. This is not the type of door that self-locks once you enter the room," says Liam.

"So someone opens an unlocked door, comes in and shoots, one time, leaves the woman alone, and takes the man's wallet and flees. Sergeant Patrick said a 911 call came in stating the woman's 'friend' had been shot. There's only one bed in this small room. Who is she to him?" asks Liam.

"I'm going to get the crime scene technicians started here. I'll notify the coroner's office for a body pickup. How about you talk with the lady who was in the room when this went down? I'll work the scene here," says Liam.

He continues to look around the room. He notices there's no luggage, no additional clothing other than what the victim had placed on the floor near his side of the bed. Liam looks into the bathroom and finds nothing, no personal items from either the victim or the surviving witness. He knocks on several doors adjacent to room 12. He speaks to Fred Tollson from Newark, New Jersey.

"Mr. Tollson, did you hear anything last night coming from room 12?"

"Yeah, I heard a loud shot, and then a male voice say something like, 'You stay here,' and something about seven hundred dollars," says Tollson.

"Did you see anyone leave the room?" asks Liam.

"No, only the woman stepping out and screaming that he's been shot."

"You said it was a few minutes until the police, fire, and ambulance got to the room. Mr. Tollson, have you stayed at this motel before?" asks Liam.

"No. This is my first, and last time, staying here. Too many single ladies walking around the front of the motel and in the parking lots. You understand what I mean?" asks Tollson.

"Did you get propositioned by a prostitute earlier tonight?" asks Liam.

"No, not me, I'm a married man. I've been married for more than thirty years. That's more time than most people do for murder these days!"

Liam walks up to the front office and speaks with Sam privately. He tells her that this woman might be a prostitute, and she may know more about this murder than she's told the first responders. Sam says,

"I ran her name, Crystal Navarro, through the local database and got a hit for an outstanding warrant for drug sales and prostitution charges. I'm going to put her in the car and talk to her more about the shooting."

"Sam, this looks like a john who got killed for his money, and she's trying to say she had no idea about what happened," says Liam. "Okay, Sam I'll continue working the scene while you work on her. I'll be just a few feet away if you need me."

"Liam, can I have the keys to the car?"

"Okay, just don't leave me here." says Liam.

Sam places Crystal in the backseat of the unmarked detective vehicle and advises her of her Miranda rights. Sam tells her she is under arrest for her outstanding warrants for drugs and prostitution charges. She tells Crystal the tall detective processing the room had located lots of evidence, including the video surveillance tape of the parking lot that shows the front door of room 12. She tells Crystal that once he sees the tape, if she was involved, she is going down for murder.

"I'm hungry," says Crystal. "I'll tell you everything if I can get some food!"

Sam calls a uniformed officer over to her vehicle. A short time later, Liam sees Sam, the uniformed officer, and Crystal drive out of the parking lot. He shakes his head, but is met at the scene by crime scene technicians. He briefs the technicians and they start the processing of the motel room for all evidence. Liam continues to assist the crime scene technicians over the next hour or so, before a coroner investigator arrives along with the body removal team. The coroner investigator uses a portable fingerprint identifier and processes the victim's prints at the scene. Liam hopes to identify the victim before he's taken to the morgue.

"I got a hit, O'Connor," says the coroner investigator. "Richard Kaufman, from Boston, a person who has been arrested for public intoxication many times. He's 64 years old, with a last known address of the South Boston Detention Facility. Sir, he appears to be a transient."

"A transient with money... seven hundred dollars," says Liam. "It's the second day of the month today, right?" asks Liam.

"Yes," says the coroner investigator.

The crime scene personnel are wrapping up their processing of the scene, and the body is loaded onto a gurney and removed from the room, when Detective Sam Masters returns with a patrol officer and Navarro. Liam looks over at Sam as they stay seated in the car, while Liam finishes up processing the motel room.

Sam gets out of the vehicle, walks over to Liam and says,

"She confessed to the whole thing."

Liam looks at Sam, smiles and says,

"Please tell me you have this all on tape?"

"Oh, that was the first thing I did. I turned the digital recorder on as soon as I put her in the back seat of our car. I told her you had the motel surveillance tape that was going to show what happened. She said she was hungry, and if I got her a couple of burgers she'd tell me everything. That's when I got the uniformed officer. I took her to McDonald's and bought her two quarter-

272

pounders with cheese, fries, and a large Coke. She ate for awhile, and then told me what she and her boyfriend did."

Liam looks at Sam and listens, but thinks to himself how proud of Sam he is.

"What did she say happened, Sam?" asks Liam.

"Crystal's a prostitute who frequently uses this motel and others up the street for her business. She told me the dead guy's name is Fred. She said he's a regular customer of hers. He lives on his Social Security check. He usually sees her at least twice a month. Once just after the first of the month, and usually a second time toward the middle. She told me it was her boyfriend's idea to rob Fred of his money. She said he needed money for drugs. She said they use meth a lot."

Sam tells Liam that Crystal stayed the whole night with Fred. The plan was that she was to service Fred, wait until he went to sleep, then Crystal would unlock the door and her boyfriend would come in and rough Fred up and steal his money. This way it would look like she had nothing to do with the robbery. "She told me she wanted to keep Fred as a trick, because he paid good. Liam, she said everything was going to plan. She got up around two-thirty in the morning, while Fred was asleep, and unlocked the front door. She said the next thing she knew, her boyfriend came busting in the room pointing a gun at Fred and her. He shot Fred once in the chest, and then took his money from his pants on the floor. She said she got scared and wanted to leave with her boyfriend, but he told her to stick with the plan and act like it was some stranger that just broke in," says Sam.

"Did she tell you where her boyfriend could be found?" asks Liam.

"She said they stay in a small trailer, in a trailer park two streets up," says Sam.

Liam, Sam, and members of the Boston Police Department arrested Luis Aguilar from a small trailer at the Lighthouse Trailer Park. Both Crystal and Luis were charged with first-degree murder. A year later, they were found guilty of all charges and sent to prison for life.

⊂◦⊃

"So, I gave Samantha the nickname 'Two Burger Sam' after that case. Sam earned some dues with that arrest and was accepted as a homicide detective. And besides, 'Two Burger Sam' was sure a lot better than what the lieutenant and other detectives wanted to call her."

"What was that?" asks Tina.

"Well, the lieutenant just wanted to call her 'S&M.' The nickname I gave her stuck, and she thanked me later when she learned what the lieutenant had come up with."

Tina and Liam finish watching the Mets game. He drives Tina back to his home. He walks her to the door and says,

"Tina, all this time you've been so nice to come over to my place. I would very much like to see where you live."

"Liam, I live in a small pool house behind a large estate. I'm fortunate the owner likes the fact I'm a cop. They're gone a lot, and I look out for the place. They don't charge much rent, but it's pretty small. I'll bring you over sometime and introduce you to my landlord," says Tina.

Liam asks Tina if she'd like to come in for a while.

"Sure, but I can't stay too long. I've got to report early in the morning to Chief Green."

He asks if she would like some coffee or something else to drink. She asks for coffee, so Liam makes a pot. Tina is impressed with his ability to navigate his way around a kitchen. The two go back to the living room and drink their coffee.

"I'm sorry it's not like my mother's, but I don't want to get you drunk," laughs Liam. "Tina, I know your chief wants me to help with the murder investigation, and I know you want to know what I'm going to do, too. I just don't know if I'm ready to go all in yet. When I work murder investigations, one hundred percent of my time and energy is devoted to solving that case. It works well for solving crimes, but it can be hard on the personal life. I care for you. I just don't want to screw things up between me and you."

"Well, Mr. Liam Matthew O'Connor, I'm a big girl. I like what I see. I've liked what I've seen since I first saw you. I'm for whatever you want."

She then reaches over and kisses Liam. She hugs him and says,

"I always feel safe with you."

Tina says she must go, even though she wants to stay longer. The timing is wrong. He walks her to the door, looks deep into her eyes and kisses her. Liam watches as Tina walks away.

After looking at four digital photos in his mind for most of the night, Liam realizes he's working the murder case already. It's 5 o'clock in the morning. Just time to shit, shower, and shave before I see Chief Green, thinks Liam. He drives to the Port Saint Lucie Police Department. It's Friday, seven in the morning. Liam talks to the on-duty officer at the front counter and asks to speak to Chief Green. He expects the chief has not arrived to work yet, and he will be unable to see him.

"Are you O'Connor, sir?" asks the desk officer.

"Yes, sir, I am," replies Liam.

"Please come this way. He was hoping you would be here early today," says the officer.

He's escorted to the chief's office and is met at the door by Chief Green.

"Good to see you, Liam," says Chief Green as he reaches out to shake his hand.

"Have a seat. Have you come to a decision, Liam?"

CPSIA information can be obtained at www.ICGtesting.com
Printed in the USA
BVOW08s1903060716

454665BV00001B/1/P